MURDER ON THE MOUNTAIN

Rosalie T. Turner with The Tuesday Breakfast Group

ISBN: 1533106843
ISBN 13: 9781533106841

Treva Baker

Treva Baker
Jacqui Binford-Bell
Alma Bock
Evelyn Bochow
Joan Bohls
Valerie Byrd *Valerie Byrd*
Lynn Coulam
Jackie Covey *Jackie Covey*
Jane Cox
Suzanne Coyle
Margie Evans
Marla Garner
D.J. Geoffroy
Sylvia Hornback *Hornback*
Becky Jones
Sarah Kangerga
Marcie Klinger
Judy MacDonald *Judy MacDonald*
Melanie Mantooth *Melanie Mantooth*
Janet Martin
MaryBeth Maxwell
Nancy Meteer
Jan Mika
Maxine Milam *Maxine Milam*
Sandra Miller
Linda Nelson
Betty Newell *Betty Newell*
Pat Pangrac
Karen Pettersen
June Rau
Vernett Safford *Vernett Safford*
Carolin Sanders
Jan Saunders

Tina Short
Susan Stuart
Camille Thomason
J.Sue Topping
Merlinda Turner
Rosalie Turner
Sherry Vacik
Doris Weaver
Mac Zimmerman

CHAPTER ONE

Morning always captured the mountain first, enfolding it in a new light, and then slipping itself into the valley. On this morning in early May, the golden dawn climbed over the mountain and shimmered its way into the Moreno Valley. The elk and deer meandered their way through the forest, occasionally pawing through the remaining snow to find some tasty morsels. Chickadees, titmice, and nuthatches twittered in the trees near those homes that had birdfeeders. Among some of the gardens, a brave crocus or daffodil was peeping out, and while lumbering across a mountain trail, an occasional bear shook itself from the lethargy of winter.

Roberta slowly opened her eyes and glanced at the clock. 5:30. In thirty minutes Al would bounce out of bed, eager for the new day and anxious to get to breakfast with the usual group, the ROMEOs, Retired Old Men Eating Out. She was glad the women, the JULIETs, Just Us Ladies Indulgently Eating Together, had the sense to change their meeting time to 9 a.m. It wasn't that Roberta wasn't someone eager for a new day; it was simply that she preferred to ease into it. She closed her eyes, sighed, and let herself slip back to sleep.

What seemed like only moments later, Roberta's eyes flew open as her alarm clock pealed out the eight o'clock hour. Al had long since gone to meet his friends for breakfast. She rose quickly and got herself ready for the day. This morning was different, though. Looking in the bathroom mirror as she brushed her brown hair, which had lots of gray, she had to admit, she could see the sadness in her eyes. In fact, her whole being seemed to carry a new weight, a new burden. With her waking she could no longer hold off the overwhelming worry that had come with their youngest daughter, Mindy's, phone call the night before.

She had known immediately when she heard Mindy's voice on the phone that something was wrong.

"Mom," Mindy had begun.

"What is it? What's wrong?" Roberta had blurted out.

"Oh, Mom, I'm so upset! I don't know what to do."

"The boys? Are the boys all right?"

"It's not the boys, Mom. We're all fine. It's…it's Ted. I told you about his gambling when I was with you all last summer, remember? Well, he said he would stop, but he hasn't. Mom, they came and repossessed his car. His car! Who knows what will go next."

"Oh, honey!"

"I can't live like this any longer. He promises to change, but he never does. I…I'm going to leave him, Mom. I…" Sobs cancelled any more words.

"Now, darling," Roberta began, wondering how to find the words to comfort her child while she, herself, was reeling from the shock the news carried with it. "Mindy, your dad and I are here for you. We'll help you through this any way we can. Do you want me to come there to Albuquerque, or do you and the boys want to come here?"

Mindy's sobs subsided somewhat. "No, not now. I made Ted leave, but the boys are devastated. It's almost the end of the school year. I hope we can stay in our house at least that long. Who knows if it will go into foreclosure? I don't have any idea of the problems his gambling debts will cause. Oh, God, how did this happen? How could Ted do this to us?"

Roberta could find no words of explanation, but her daughter had rushed on anyway. "Remember when we were there last month? That night when Ted left and I didn't know where he'd gone? He acted so strange when he got back, so, I don't know, nervous or something. I asked him if he'd been gambling, but he denied it. He swore he wasn't gambling, and I believed him. I thought maybe he'd just gone for a drive wanting some time alone, but he must have gone to Taos to the casino or something and lost a lot of money. Oh, Mom!"

Roberta and Al had taken turns talking to their daughter, listening to her broken heart, hoping they could help in some way. Later the two of them had talked long into the night after the phone call. "How could Ted gamble away everything?" they asked each other over and over. There was never an answer.

"I can't imagine that Ted would do this," first Roberta, then Al would say, "Ted has been such a good father, so involved with the boys." They shook their heads over and over, trying to get past the feeling of being ambushed. Roberta made them both a cup of hot milk with some Ovaltine stirred in, something her mother had done for her when, as a child, she'd wake from a bad dream.

It had been a long night for both Al and Roberta. They lay awake for a long time, their concern for their daughter almost a physical pain. Their hands would touch and clasp, speaking the silent language of a long marriage. Finally, they both had crossed into sleep.

At least now there was a plan. At the end of the school year, Mindy, nine-year-old Scott and seven-year-old Walker would move to Angel Fire and stay with Al and Roberta, at least temporarily.

Mindy's job as a graphic designer made it possible for her to work from home.

Roberta moved on to the kitchen and snatched her keys off the key rack by the garage door. She knew she would share Mindy's plight with her friends at breakfast, as they'd shared so many things throughout the years, and she knew she would find some comfort with that sharing.

The temperature hadn't gotten above freezing during the night, but the sun was bright on a cloudless day so the morning held the promise of warmth. Even so, Roberta wore her heavy navy jacket and draped a woolen scarf around her neck before pulling on her lined gloves. She pulled into Kay's driveway, the "mud season" roads splattering brown flecks as she drove.

Kay was ready, as always, and appeared immediately in her stylish red coat, plaid scarf and black leather gloves. Her well-cut gray hair was fluffed attractively around her perfectly made-up face, her green eyes shining brightly. She seemed to have completely recovered from the loss of her friend, Ed, who had died tragically last year in a car wreck. Sherry Sullivan had been seriously injured in that accident also, but she, too, seemed to have recovered. The fact that Sherry and Ed had been together had been a difficult truth for Kay to face.

Roberta and Kay drove the short distance to the newly opened Firefly Café, making small talk as they went. Kay's glances at her friend, however, let Roberta know that Kay was aware something was wrong. As she pulled into a parking space in front of the restaurant, Roberta looked at Kay. "I'll tell you all about it when everyone gets there, OK?"

Kay nodded, turned and opened the car door, and jumped out to avoid the nearest mud puddle. Tessa had already arrived, and the smell of coffee welcomed them into the warmth. Tessa's long, dark hair was pulled back in its usual ponytail, and that style emphasized the classic beauty of her face, the deep brown eyes, the high cheekbones, and aquiline nose. As the most athletic of the group her streamlined body radiated energy. Olivia soon swished through the door in her usual, hurried manner. Her blonde, curly, flyaway hair made her look even more frenzied.

"Amazing!" she exclaimed. "I'm not the last one here. Where's Myra?"

The others shrugged. "Probably delivering a casserole to some hapless soul," Kay remarked.

"Now, Kay," began Roberta; however, she smiled along with the others. Myra's unending casserole-giving was legendary in the community.

Just then, Myra arrived, somewhat resembling a large marshmallow in her white, padded coat. Her gray pageboy hairstyle framed her round face, and her blue eyes glanced over the group of friends as if taking attendance.

"Myra," said Tessa, "we were wondering where you were. You're usually the first one here."

"I would have been here sooner, but there was some kind of commotion at Monte Verde Lake when I went by. I wanted to see what was going on, but the police made me move on."

"What do you mean? What kind of commotion?" asked Kay.

"I couldn't tell. There was a rescue vehicle, the fire truck, and two police vehicles. I tried to get J.D.'s attention, but he waved me on. I thought maybe a deer or elk had gotten stuck in the lake again, but I couldn't see anything."

"Well, if it's anything important, in this village we'll find out soon enough." Roberta said. "I remember when that deer fell through the ice and the firemen rescued her. Now, at least, we have that special equipment for lake rescues."

"And we have the best emergency people anywhere. I've never heard anything but lots of praise for them. Every now and then I'll take a casserole or some cookies or something down to them. They need to know we appreciate them," said Myra.

The friends smiled at Myra as the server came to the table. The group placed their orders and sat quietly for a moment. Kay looked at Roberta and raised her eyebrows, questioning.

Roberta sighed. "I want to share something with you all, something that is breaking my heart."

The friends set down their coffee cups and waited.

"Mindy, our youngest, called last night. Her husband evidently has had a real gambling problem for a long time. She discovered it last year and begged him to stop, and he said he would, but he hasn't. They repossessed his car yesterday, and Mindy has decided that they must separate. When school ends, she'll move here temporarily with the boys."

"Oh, Bertie," said Kay. "I am so sorry."

Roberta bit her bottom lip and willed the tears that filled her eyes to stop. "It's such a shock. Ted is a nice guy, a wonderful father. I can't begin to imagine how much this will hurt Scott and Walker. How could Ted be so stupid as to jeopardize his wonderful family…"

"It's hard to understand about gambling," said Myra. "It's a kind of addiction. Maybe if he got some counseling, he could stop."

"I'm hoping that the separation might shock him into the need to do something about it. I can't believe he'd let his family fall apart."

Tessa nodded. "We'll all hope for that, Bertie."

"And you know you all will be in my prayers," said Kay, whose faith was a strong part of her very core. "There's strength in prayer power."

Roberta took a deep breath. "I wanted to tell you all, share it with you. But, now, let's talk about something else. Something pleasant."

"If it helps any, I have to say that my nephew seems to have completely redeemed himself. Remember that Tony stole some of my paintings to pay off his gambling debts last year. I feel sure he will never gamble like that again, and he's paid me back every penny," Olivia said.

"He also cut and stacked all your wood for this winter, didn't he?" asked Tessa.

"He sure did. And he's taking up mountain biking in a big way, so I'm sure he'll be coming to Angel Fire a lot. We have become such a great place for mountain biking here."

"That is one sport I can't understand," said Myra. "What fun can there be in hurtling down a rocky mountain path on a flimsy few metal bars with wheels. Scares me to death to think of it."

Kay laughed. "Me, too, Myra. There are so many other nice, sedate sports for us old-timers, like golf, or hiking."

"You're not an old-timer," said Tessa. "You should try pickleball with us sometime. Jim and I love it, and it's become so popular here in Angel Fire."

The orders came, and conversation was interrupted while coffee cups were refilled.

"Want some more hot water for your tea?" the server asked Tessa.

"No, thanks. This is fine." She took a sip, enjoying her herbal tea.

"I love that it's almost spring and I can soon get out and find some new scene to paint," said Olivia. "Winter is beautiful here, but I love the spring and summer. And the fall, too. Actually, I guess I love all of it." She smiled.

Roberta nodded. "I like knowing that all our friends that are here only part-time will be back soon."

"I wonder if Wanda has found a new supply of tee shirts with those funny sayings. I love seeing those every Tuesday morning."

"Some of them are just ridiculous," muttered Myra.

"That's what makes them fun," responded Kay. "By the way, since it will soon be the end of the school year, what's going to happen to your boarders in that downstairs apartment? I remember you told them they could stay through Shandra's senior year. She'll graduate this month, won't she?"

"Yes, and I hate to see them leave. I've felt so much better knowing someone was down there. Shandra is graduating at the top of her class and has received several scholarships and will be going to school back in Texas, near where Hannah's parents live. Hannah always planned to go back after her husband left them, but wanted Shandra to finish her senior year here."

"That was such a hard time for them," commented Roberta. "You were so generous to take them in, Myra."

"Nonsense. Anyone would have done the same. I happened to have that empty apartment, and they were living in their car. It worked out for all of us."

"Will you start renting out that apartment now?" asked Tessa.

"I don't know. I'll have to think about it. Maybe I'll find someone else who needs a helping hand."

"I wish we could help contribute to Shandra's education fund," said Tessa. "She and her mom have worked so hard for that."

"Maybe we could do some kind of a fund-raiser," said Roberta. "What's a popular way to raise some money these days? Maybe a yard sale?"

"Bake sales always do well here. People who aren't used to the altitude don't like to bake because of the changes you have to make to the recipes. I bet we could put a table at Lowe's and sell a lot of baked goods," suggested Kay.

Myra slapped the table. "A cookbook! Everybody loves a cookbook. We're all good cooks and have lots of recipes we could put in it. Why, I've got dozens of casserole recipes I'd love to share."

"That's a great idea," said Olivia. "Let's make a cookbook. We can get ideas from the others, Wanda and Annabelle, and any of those that come in for the summer."

Roberta pulled a notebook and pen from her purse, and the ladies began making plans.

The restaurant door burst open and several men bustled in, talking excitedly among themselves.

"Morning, guys. What's going on?" asked Nathaniel, one of Firefly's owners.

The tallest of the group pulled off his cap and ran his fingers through his hair. "They just pulled a body out of the lake, a woman. All we know is she's dead. Could be an accident, or suicide, or, maybe even a murder."

"A murder?" The five women looked at each other, shock registering in each set of eyes.

CHAPTER TWO

For several weeks the sketchy details of the woman pulled from the lake filled almost every conversation in the Moreno Valley. The horror of a death, whether murder, accidental, or a suicide, which ended in the cold, murky water shocked the hearts of the locals and tweaked the interest of any visitors. Who was she? How did it happen? Was there a murderer on the loose? Many had questions, without real answers. The coverage in the *Wheeler Peak Press* or the online *Sangre de Cristo Chronicle*, or even in the *Taos News*, didn't give the answers everyone was looking for. People talked about it with George at the barber shop and Tess and Andrea at the post office.

There was some information, of course. A name: Beverly Tensley. Her age: 37. She was single, living in a cabin at the Bobcat Meadows RV Park between Eagle Nest and Red River; the park that had a few cabins in addition to RV spaces. She had moved most recently from Albuquerque where she had worked as a dealer in casinos. She was known as a quiet person who kept to herself. To date, there was no known family. The cause of death was still undetermined, awaiting toxicology and other forensic reports. Speculation ran rampant until, finally, people became more interested in when the golf course would open, what kind of summer season there might be, what new restaurants would open, and how much worse the pot holes in the roads were getting to be.

On Tuesday morning, Roberta and Kay arrived at breakfast with the latest stack of recipes for the cookbook in hand. After the group had ordered, they compared notes.

"This is the best chicken pot pie recipe I've ever tried," commented Kay. "We definitely have to include it."

Myra nodded. "I agree, but we have to be careful not to have too many chicken recipes. I've already included six chicken casseroles. We need some different things."

"True," said Olivia. "How are we doing on desserts and side dishes?"

Roberta counted those on her list. "We could use more of those for balance, especially vegetable kinds of things."

Tessa looked through the papers she had brought. "I have some organic dishes I want to include. In fact, I think we should have a special section for that. You know, include some things like local wild mushrooms, greens, and stuff."

"Good idea," said Kay. "That reminds me about something I heard about the dead woman. I was eating lunch over in Eagle Nest and the people at the next table were talking. I wasn't eavesdropping, but I couldn't help overhearing."

The four friends looked at Kay expectantly.

"One of the ladies lived in the cabin near the woman who died. She was telling the others at the table how that woman was a real nature lover, how she knew everything about the natural plants that grow wild around here, like those mushrooms. What are they called? Chantrells, or something?"

Tessa nodded. "Yes, Chanterelles."

"Anyway, she told how that woman would use all those things in her meals. She, the dead woman I mean, and this lady that was telling about it, would go hiking together and she would say things like, 'These berries are good for this or that, but don't ever eat this kind of berry.' She sounds like she was a very interesting person."

"I would have loved to have known her," said Tessa. "I can't help wondering about her and what happened. Do you think we'll ever know?"

Myra shrugged. "I'm not hearing about any progress on the case."

"Well, if you don't have any information, Myra, nobody in this valley has any." Kay picked up her toast and smiled at Myra before she took a bite.

"Of course, since it's a death, the case is under the state trooper investigators. Our local police aren't the ones heading up the investigation. I saw J.D. at Cowboy Fellowship last week, but he didn't say anything about it," Myra said.

Their talk drifted to their usual topics, what was happening on the news, who had already come in for the summer season, and the latest books they had read. Roberta was reminded again of how easily conversation flowed between them even though there were such differences between them as far as age, background, and interests. *That's the way women are,* she thought. *And I'm glad it's that way.*

May warmed its way into the valley, and with it came the early visitors arriving for the summer season. May also marked the end of the school year, and the JULIETs gathered with the proud parents, grandparents, and friends of the high school grads. They sat together, chatting in their usual manner, as they waited for the ceremony to begin at the Moreno Valley High School.

"When are Hannah and Shandra leaving?" asked Olivia.

"They plan to head back to Texas on Monday," answered Myra. "I sure do hate to see them go."

"But you made this year such a good one for them, Myra," said Roberta. "They were very lucky."

Myra squirmed a little in her chair. "By the way, I told them about our cookbook project. I said that at the end of the summer we'd have a contribution to send them to go towards Shandra's books or something. They were touched by that, I think."

A stirring from the rear of the room brought silence to the crowd. The pep band began playing as the graduates processed in wearing their black gowns with light blue stoles. The JULIETs exchanged a few bemused glances when, instead of the traditional "Pomp and Circumstance," the band burst into "A Punk" by Vampire Weekend, at least that's what it said it was on the program. The Interim Director, Doug Wine, welcomed everyone to the ceremonies. A highlight was the Dedications, when each of the seniors gave a short talk about their high school experience, and thanked special teachers or persons. The JULIETs were pleased that Shandra thought to include Myra in her thanks. Hannah smiled over at the JULIETs after Shandra gave her dedication, and each of them was thinking about Myra's unconditional generosity.

As Shandra walked across and received her diploma, Roberta glanced at Myra and smiled to herself as she noted Myra's expression of joy and pride, and saw a single tear slip down Myra's cheek. *Myra, who loves to be brusque and crusty, is a big creampuff at heart,* she thought to herself.

Jim and Tessa chose the day to hike the Bull Springs Meadow Trail. Their rescue dog, Wilbur, padded along beside them. Wild iris carpeted the area as they neared the high point. The deep blue of the unique New Mexico sky made a canopy over them. Tessa paused and savored the view, the breeze ruffling the tendrils around her face left escaping from her long ponytail.

Jim stopped and turned. "Are you tired?" he asked.

"No. Sometimes I need to stop and marvel at this beautiful place." She took a deep breath, filling her senses with the fresh mountain air. Wilbur took advantage of the lull to plop down beside Tessa.

Jim walked the few paces back to where his wife stood and looked back over the valley. The ponderosa pines stood majestically along the ridge, the sunlight glinting on the reddish bark. The aspens spilled throughout the hillsides, their forest green leaves whispering in the wind. Above the subtle sounds of the forest there was a profound silence, a cathedral silence.

"Sometimes," Tessa began, "I don't know. Sometimes, I feel so lucky to be me, to be able to live here, to have you for my husband, I…it's almost scary."

Jim laughed and pulled her to him, kissing her on her forehead. "You mean like that old Kris Kristofferson song, "What did I ever do to deserve even one of the blessings I've known?"

"You always turn everything into a country-western song."

"Of course. Country-western songs explain life, don't they?"

Tessa was silent for a moment. "Jim," she said, turning to look him in the face. "Do you ever wish we'd had children?"

Jim smiled at his wife. "We've discussed this a million times, Tess. It's the way things are. I'm fine about it. Aren't you?"

"Yes, it's only that it seems selfish. I mean, there are children who need homes. We could provide a wonderful home. Maybe we should look into being foster parents."

Jim took her hand and turned back to start up the trail. "That's a huge responsibility. If you want to look into it, though, I'm OK with that. But, now, let's get on with our hike. Come on, Wilbur, up you go."

Roberta woke in the middle of the night to the sound of rain gently tapping on their metal roof. She tossed and turned for a few minutes before giving up. She looked at Al, who seemed to be in a deep sleep, and she envied him that ability. Ever since Mindy's phone call, Roberta's nights were often disturbed. She slipped out of bed and made her way to the living room, quietly shutting the bedroom door behind her.

The full moon wasn't able to peep through the clouds but she still had enough light to make her way to Al's recliner. She gathered up the afghan from the sofa on her way and wrapped it around herself as she curled up in the chair. *We never stop being parents,* she thought, *no matter how old our kids get to be.* For the hundredth time, she went over and over Mindy's situation, wondering what she could possibly do to fix it.

The bedroom door opened and Al padded out. "I thought you might be sitting out here." What's wrong? Thinking about our girl?"

Roberta nodded. She moved to the sofa to sit by her husband. "My heart is breaking over this," she said. "Being separated from their dad is going to hurt Scott and Walker so much. I'm furious with Ted! I want to shake him and make him come to his senses."

Al put his arm around his wife and she leaned against him, finding some comfort in his familiar strength. He sighed. "And I'd like to horsewhip him. I wish we didn't like him so much."

"Mmm. I have trouble remembering that. At least they're going to counseling. That's a start."

"Yes, but I'm glad Mindy's still planning on moving here in June. The separation might be what he needs to realize that he has to get the addiction under control. It will be good for the boys to be here for the summer. We'll keep them busy."

"Sure. There's so much for them here in the summer. I checked the schedule and they'll get here in time for the Missoula Children's Theater. That is such a great program and I think they'll enjoy it."

The two sat in silence for a while. "Think you might be able to get back to sleep, Bertie?" asked Al, stifling a yawn.

"Not quite yet. You go on back to bed, though."

"OK. Don't stay up too long." He kissed her cheek and left her to her thoughts.

The rain stopped and the lavender-gray clouds moved across the sky. Roberta snuggled a little deeper into the afghan and watched as the clouds were tinged with silver when they slipped past the moon. She wondered if her daughter was able to sleep, or if she was sitting up watching the same full moon. *If she is, I hope she's feeling the love I'm sending her way. If only a mother's love could make a difference.* She wiped the tears from her eyes and made her way back to bed.

At breakfast on Tuesday morning, Roberta had all the pages of the cookbook put in order. She was glad for this project to help take her mind off her family's problems, but she knew she'd better get it wrapped up before Mindy and the boys moved in next week. "Now, do you think these are enough recipes? Annabelle and Wanda each sent me several. We can still add some more before I send it to the printer. We do need to hurry and get it out so we can sell a lot this summer, though."

Kay opened her purse and brought out a piece of paper. "I came across this old recipe for ham loaf this week, one of Laura Vance's recipes. It's pretty good. Can you add one more?"

"Sure," said Roberta. "Any others?"

The four women shook their heads.

Olivia's phone chimed and she pulled it from her pocket, checking the message. "Oh, it's from my nephew, Tony. He and some friends will be up this weekend for the mountain bike races. I told him they could all camp out at my place."

"I'm so glad that business with him from last year got all cleared up," said Roberta.

"Me, too," responded Olivia.

Tessa turned to Kay. "I saw you at the golf course this week. There was someone I didn't recognize in your foursome and I wondered who it was."

Kay blushed slightly and picked up her coffee cup quickly. "Oh, no one. I mean, our fourth couldn't play so they paired him up with us. His name is Ben James. He moved here recently. He's a retired Methodist minister." She took a sip of coffee.

"Well?" said Myra, her voice a question.

"Well, what?" asked Kay.

"Is he nice? What's he like? Did you like him? Has he got a family? Come on, Kay, tell us everything."

"I didn't have him fill out a questionnaire, for goodness sake! I think he's a widower. He's from somewhere in Texas. I think he has grown children there."

Silence descended for a moment as the four friends studied Kay.

She looked at them all, and exasperation showed on her face. "What? Why are you all making so much out of this?"

Myra, of course, kept pushing. "Are you going to see him again?"

"Myra! Enough. We may play Bridge together this week, but we'll see. It's not definite. Now, I don't want to hear any more about this."

The group exchanged knowing glances and smiles and, wisely, moved on to their usual topics of books and local activities.

The first weekend in June promised beautiful weather for the mountain bike races. Tony arrived at Olivia's early on Friday afternoon.

"Auntie, hello!" Tony greeted his aunt with a bear hug and kiss as she opened the door. "Thanks for letting us stay here."

Olivia looked beyond him to the driveway. "Where are the others?" she asked.

"They're coming up in another car. We couldn't fit all the bikes and gear in my car. They should be here soon. They were ready to leave right after me."

Tony brought in his duffle bag and another bag filled with pads, helmet, tools, bike chains, and who knew what else from the looks of it.

"That's a lot of stuff," Olivia remarked. She smiled at Tony as she showed him where to stash everything.

"I've learned this is an expensive sport," said Tony. "Of course, I got everything second-hand, but my friends have poured the money into it. Some of the bikes cost $10,000 or more."

"Ten thousand dollars! How can they afford that while going to college?"

"Well, the two guys I bike with are finished with college and are working. Neither has a wife or kids yet, plus they both come from families with money. I'm lucky they hang out with me."

"Tony, you're not getting in over your head again, are you?"

Tony laughed and hugged his aunt. "No, Aunt Olivia, I promise you I've learned my lesson about that. I go over all my finances with Dad and Mom now."

Olivia looked at her nephew with a skeptical expression on her face.

Tony held up his hands. "Honest, Aunt Olivia."

Olivia smiled. "OK. I believe you. Let's go sit on the patio and visit until your friends get here. I fixed chicken enchiladas for supper and all I have to do is heat them up."

An hour later Tony looked at his watch in surprise. "They should have been here by now. Let me give them a call and see what the delay is." He pulled his cell phone out of his pocket and punched in a number. When the call went to voice mail he left a message, and then tried another number with the same result.

"That's strange," he said, looking at Olivia with a worried frown on his face.

"They're probably between here and Taos. Most people don't have cell phone service through the canyon."

Tony nodded. "Yeah, I guess so. That means they'll be here within a half hour or so."

The two sat in comfortable conversation as the evening slipped around them. They watched several deer grazing nearby. Every so often Tony tried to call his friends again, always with it going to voicemail.

The shadows grew deeper and the clouds turned from mauve to purple to gray. The light faded and the silence of sundown filled the spaces. After another two hours, Tony got up and started pacing. "Something's wrong, Aunt Olivia. Something's very wrong."

CHAPTER THREE

One look at her nephew's worried expression sent a chill down Olivia's back. She was beginning to get a bad sense about the situation herself. "Why don't you call our local police and see if there's been an accident. If there hasn't been, maybe you should tell them that you're worried about your friends." She got up and walked toward her desk. "I'll get you their non-emergency number. We have a good police force here. I'm sure they'll help you figure out what's wrong."

"Yeah, I'd better do that." Tony took the cordless phone from his aunt as she looked up the number.

Olivia went into the kitchen while Tony made the call and turned on the oven to heat up the enchiladas. She poured herself a glass of wine, a Merlot she'd been wanting to try.

"What did they say?" she asked as Tony came into the kitchen and set the phone down.

"They're checking between here and Albuquerque, but they hadn't heard of any accident. I kind of think they suspect the guys stopped off for drinks somewhere, but I know these guys wouldn't do a lot of drinking the night before the bike races. They're too serious about the races for that. Anyway, the officer was real nice. He's going to call me back and let me know."

"Do you think you should call your friends' parents?"

Tony shook his head. "No, at least not yet. The guys don't live at home."

Moments later the phone rang, and after answering it, Olivia passed it to Tony.

"Yes, sir. …Nothing? Well, thank you for checking…. What do you think I should do?....Yes, sir. I understand….Thank you."

Tony hung up the phone and stood quietly, his hand resting on the receiver. "No accidents." He turned to his aunt, his expression full of concern. "They said there's nothing I can do until more time passes. I don't know, Aunt Olivia. I guess I can only wait, but I'm really worried."

"I know you are, hon, but I'm sure there's a logical explanation. Let's have some supper and see what happens." She went to the refrigerator and pulled out the ingredients for a salad.

"This is too weird," Tony said the next morning as he seemed to inhale the bacon and eggs Olivia had made for him. "I still can't get any answer and I haven't heard anything from them."

"Are you going to go ahead and race today?" Olivia asked.

"I don't know what to do! I feel guilty racing if something's happened to them, but if they're goofing off somewhere and I miss a chance to race here, I'll really be mad. What do you think I should do, Aunt Olivia?"

Olivia shrugged. "I think you should probably go ahead and race. There has to be some logical explanation. What worries me, though, is what if you're so distracted by all this that you're not concentrating on the race. That's when accidents happen, and, Tony, I don't want you to have any kind of accident."

Smiling at his aunt, Tony answered. "Believe me, when I start to race I am so focused nothing could distract me."

"Well, you're here anyway so I think you should race. In case you end up hanging out with the others there, I'll be going out around 4:30 to meet friends at the country club for drinks and maybe dinner. One of our good friends that we have breakfast with got here this week with her husband, Annabelle and Phillip Barron. There are leftovers in the refrigerator if you want to eat here. I won't be late."

Roberta and Al picked up Kay on their way to the country club and arrived at the same time as Jim and Tessa Garcia. They made their way to the lounge and joined Myra, then pushed the tables along the wall together. When Annabelle and Phillip arrived they were greeted with hugs of welcome.

"Annabelle, how was your winter?" asked Roberta.

"It was wonderful, thanks. Of course, at my age just waking up and being able to get out of bed makes a person feel good."

Roberta took in her friend's tall, slim body dressed stylishly in black slacks and a flowing black tunic, flowered cane discreetly by her side, her silver-white hair smoothed back and held with a wide silver clasp, her bright blue eyes that held a twinkle, and she marveled at how Annabelle always looked so perfectly put together. It was more than outward appearance though, Roberta thought. Annabelle exuded a calmness, a serenity of spirit that many people lacked. It was this characteristic that Roberta most admired.

The men began immediately talking sports as they clustered at one end of the tables.

"Did you take any trips this year?" asked Tessa.

"I had the most wonderful trip," began Annabelle. "First, Phillip and I drove to the little town where I grew up. We went all over my family's ranch, and I simply steeped myself in my memories, then later I spent a week at a monastery on a personal retreat."

"Sounds wonderful," said Kay.

Tessa looked at her older friend with a slightly puzzled expression on her face. "I didn't know you grew up on a ranch, Annabelle. I remember you said once you grew up in a small town, but you are so 'Dallas' that I forget that. But, out on a ranch? That I can't picture."

Annabelle laughed her quiet laugh. "Yes, I was quite the cowgirl. I wanted to be with my dad wherever he was, so I'd go along on roundups and brandings and the whole thing. While I was back there this time I remembered all those times, all the important lessons one learns in that rough world of survival, as well as the gentle lessons I learned from my very southern mother."

"Do you still have family on the ranch?" asked Kay.

"Oh, no. My father died when I was thirteen, and we had to sell the ranch and move to town."

"That must have been a difficult time," said Myra. "I...."

Olivia swept into the room and rushed to greet everyone and give a special hug to Annabelle. "I'm sorry I'm late. My nephew, Tony, is here for the bike races, but his friends never showed up. We've been so worried. I was waiting at home in case he'd heard something, but he must have decided to stay and eat with some of the other racers."

"What do you think happened?" asked Roberta.

"We have no idea. He can't reach them on their cell phones. They were supposed to be right behind him yesterday. I think if he hasn't heard anything yet he may have gone to the police. I'm anxious to know. Anyway, I'm glad to be here now and see you again, Annabelle."

The server came to the table and took their drink orders. By now the men's conversation had moved on to their golf games.

"Annabelle was telling us about growing up on a ranch. She went back this summer and she also went to a monastery. I want to hear about that." Myra leaned forward now that the men's conversation grew a little louder. Even though football season was months away, the TCU fans were already fired up about the upcoming year.

"My retreat at the monastery you mean?" said Annabelle. "There's not much to tell. I believe that we all need time to leave the routine of daily life and reflect on where we are and, also, on where we might be going. We need to revisit our very selves, perhaps."

"I would love that," said Tessa. "Don't we all have some issues we need quiet time to deal with?"

"I don't know," began Myra.

Olivia glanced up and saw Tony at the doorway. She raised her hand and waved. "Over here, Tony."

He hurried to the table. "Excuse me. I'm sorry to barge in, but Aunt Olivia, I have to talk to you."

"You can talk here, Tony. I told my friends the story."

He pulled out his phone. "I just saw this online. I have this app, see?" He clicked a couple of buttons on his phone. "It alerts me when there might be a good deal for a mountain bike or biking supplies on eBay. This came up a few minutes ago." He showed Olivia a picture of a mountain bike.

"And, so?" she asked, looking at him with a puzzled frown.

"So," he exclaimed, "I know this is Ryan's bike. It had some distinctive things on it."

"You mean he's selling his bike and giving up racing?"

"No, Auntie! I mean someone else put up this ad. Someone else is selling his bike!"

Oliva looked around at her friends, then back at Tony. "I don't understand."

Annabelle leaned toward Tony. "You think someone has stolen this bike, and perhaps done something to your friend?"

"Exactly!"

"I think it's time to go to the police." said Annabelle.

Olivia got up quickly and grabbed her purse. I'll go with you."
She pulled a ten dollar bill and tossed it on the table.

"Text us and let us know what happens," called Roberta to
Olivia's disappearing back.

"How disturbing," said Kay. "I hope everything turns out OK."

Al paused in his conversation and greeted a nice-looking man
who had entered the room. He was of average height with graying
hair and bright blue eyes. His trim physique indicated someone
who had been athletic all his life. "Come join us," Al urged. "Let
me introduce you to everyone. This is Ben James. He's recently
moved to our village. We met at the golf course yesterday."

Myra glanced at Kay and back at the newcomer.

As Al made all the introductions, Ben said, "I've already had
the pleasure of meeting Kay. I got to be paired with her group
when I didn't know anyone here yet." He gave a smile and nod in
her direction.

Kay could feel the buzz of interest flying around her friends
like a busy, annoying bee. She wanted to glare at them, but, to her
surprise, that feeling quickly left and she simply felt amused. Let
them think whatever they wanted. She had only recently met the
man, for heaven's sake! He could be a serial killer for all they knew.
Of course, that wasn't likely of a Methodist minister, was it?

The group resettled itself with the addition of Ben, and the
conversation became more general than gender-divided since everyone wanted to get to know the newcomer.

After ordering a glass of wine, he began to answer the questions thrown his way. His relaxed manner telegraphed his open,
friendly nature to the group.

"You know how it is with Methodist ministers," he said. "We get
moved around a lot, although I stayed in Texas and New Mexico
the whole time."

Tessa smiled. "And there's a lot of room in Texas to move
around in."

"For sure. I retired four years ago, and my wife and I came up here to Angel Fire a few times. We loved it. My wife died a year and a half ago. Cancer."

Kay noticed a sadness pass fleetingly over his face, and it touched a place inside her where she hid the same pain.

"Anyway, I didn't like kicking around in that big, empty house, so I gathered our three kids and told them I needed to do something different and I planned to move up here. They were all for it. They love to come up here with their families. So, here I am." His smile took in each one of the group, and they smiled back.

"We're glad you're here, Ben." said Al. "Have you visited the United Church of Angel Fire yet?"

"My wife and I did when we came up, and I'm looking forward to attending from now on. That church has an interesting background with four founding denominations. It really speaks for ecumenicalism."

Roberta nodded. "And we have at least twelve different denominations attending now, and it doesn't matter which anyone is. Our motto is 'Divine Love in Action,' and that's what we try to be all about."

"That's wonderful," said Ben.

"So, who's your favorite football team?" asked Jim.

Myra rolled her eyes. "Sports. Always sports," she muttered, shaking her head. The men had already turned toward each other.

"They don't know how to talk about anything else, poor things," said Roberta.

Tessa's cell phone chimed and she dug it out of her purse. Studying it for a moment she said, "It's Olivia. The police have contacted the parents and the young men are now considered missing persons. All the police between here and Albuquerque are on alert for them." She looked at her friends. "That's a huge area. How will they ever find them?"

The others remained silent for a moment, each one wondering what could have possibly happened to make two young men disappear. Then they each thought of their own families and how terrifying this must be for the parents of those young men.

Roberta turned toward Annabelle and said, "You were going to tell us about your time at the monastery."

Annabelle smiled. "I like to have some kind of personal retreat every few years. It helps me to remember what is really important to me, that kind of thing. Doing that clears my mind of all the busyness that slips in so easily."

Tessa's phone chimed again. She read the text and a puzzled look appeared on her face. "Listen to this. It's from Olivia. Tony just got a text from his friend's phone, obviously not from his friend. It said, 'If you want to see your fellow racers again, think copper and gold.' What could that possibly mean?"

"Copper could be another word for a policeman, but I don't think that's what they mean here. I think they mean the actual metals of copper and gold, don't you?" said Myra.

"Yes. It could mean coins, you know, copper pennies and gold coins. That's some kind of clue about where those boys are," added Kay.

"Think about those two metals, copper and gold, that's the clue," said Annabelle. "Let's look at the big picture. The boys could be anywhere between here and Albuquerque. What place in that range of space makes you think about copper and gold together?"

"One of the casinos?" suggested Myra.

Annabelle frowned. "Maybe. But how could two young men be hidden in a casino?"

"Elizabethtown!" exclaimed Roberta. "That was the town developed because of the gold rush on Mount Baldy."

"Yes, that's a possibility. Maybe the boys are captive somewhere in Elizabethtown."

"But there's nothing there but that one family, and I'm sure they wouldn't be involved in any robbery or kidnapping," said Kay.

"Do you remember when we were in the Historical Society, years ago when Jack Urban headed it up?" Annabelle asked. Kay and Roberta nodded. "He taught us so much about this area. I think the answer lies at Baldy. That's where the copper and gold were first found."

Tessa leaned forward. "Yes, I remember when Jim and I explored all up in that area!" Her voice carried her excitement. "We came across some old miners' cabins. The boys might be up there. What was the name of that?" She drummed her fingers on the table. "Something Gulch. Jim," she called to the other end of the table. "What was the name of that gulch opposite Elizabethtown that we hiked up and found those miners' cabins?"

Her husband looked at her in confusion.

"Think, Jim. It's important. A few years ago we explored all around Mount Baldy."

Jim's puzzled expression cleared. "Oh, yeah. That was...hold on, it's coming to me. Gulch. It was Pine Gulch. We went up it and it ended at that little lake."

"Yes! Good job, honey." She blew a kiss his way. Tessa snatched up her phone and her thumbs flew as she put in the message. When she finished she smiled at the women. "I told Olivia to suggest the police look up there. It would be the perfect place to hold someone hostage."

"Wow," said Myra. "That is some pretty good detective work from us. We might want to hire out to the police department as investigators."

"Of course, that's assuming we're right," remarked Kay.

"Let's hope we are, and this nightmare for those families can end. Maybe we'll find out in the morning," said Roberta.

"Hey, do you ladies want to order dinner now?" asked Al from the other end of the table.

"We're ready," said Roberta.

The evening moved on; the wall-mounted TV showing a base-ball game; conversations making a thrumming noise above the clink of dishes and silverware; and, among the JULIETs, impatient glances at watches and phones and silent prayers for the safety of some young men they didn't even know.

CHAPTER FOUR

E ven though the JULIETs had already discussed every aspect of
the stunning results of their detective work over the weekend,
it was the first topic of conversation when Kay got in Roberta's car
Tuesday morning.

"I could hardly believe it when Olivia texted us all about the
police finding those boys in the miners' cabins. What would have
happened if we hadn't figured it out?" Kay said.

"I expect they could have eventually broken out even with
those bars nailed across the door. Obviously, the robbers didn't
want them to die since they left them water and some food."

"I don't call a bag of trail mix food," scoffed Kay.

Roberta gently braked the car as two prairie dogs scurried
across the road.

"You know some people are actually aiming for those little var-
mints," noted Kay. "Prairie dogs have taken over Angel Fire."

"I know," said Roberta, "but I can't make myself deliberately
kill one."

Kay smiled. "I can't either. The Smiths were due back Sunday. I hope Wanda is at breakfast."

"I'm pretty sure she'll be there. She won't want to miss a single one of our get-togethers."

"I can't wait to tell her how we solved the crime and saved two young men. I wonder if they'll ever catch the kidnappers."

Roberta pulled into a parking place. "According to Olivia, the robbers wore stocking masks, ski caps and gloves the whole time so the boys aren't sure they could identify them. She said the police think they're part of a ring that deals with those expensive mountain bikes and that they'll eventually be caught."

The two got out of the car and went inside, greeting Wanda with a welcoming hug as they got to their table.

"This is wonderful. Wanda and Annabelle are back in the fold so we're all together again. It's going to be a great summer," exclaimed Roberta.

"Yes, and we can all get our dose of wisdom from Wanda's tee shirts," muttered Myra.

Wanda stood and displayed her latest which said, "I Dream of a Society Where a Chicken Can Cross the Road Without Its Motives Questioned."

As she sat down she said, "OK. Bring me up to date. Tell me everything that's going on."

Olivia, Kay and Myra all began talking at once.

"Whoa!" Wanda said. "One at a time."

"Olivia should tell it," said Annabelle. "It's really her story."

Their server came to the table and everyone placed their orders. As soon as she left, Annabelle nodded at Olivia.

Olivia smiled at her and recounted, detail by detail, what had happened to the mountain bikers and all the JULIETs had done to help find them. She finished by summarizing the details she'd learned at the police station after the officers had brought the boys safely in. "Evidently, this ring watches when there's going to be a mountain bike event somewhere. They must have scouted the road to find the best place to stop the boys, at least that's what the police think. They pick a car that has two boys and two bikes, then they pass them and gesture to pull over, like something is wrong with their bikes. It's always some isolated stretch of road. There's four kidnappers. Tony's friends said they all get out of the vehicles, and while the guys are checking their bikes, they put a handkerchief with chloroform over their noses and mouths and dump them in the kidnappers' van. One of the kidnappers takes the keys and drives the car with the bikes to Albuquerque to sell. They wipe down the car of any trace and abandon it somewhere. The others took the boys to one of those abandoned cabins, and that's where they left them. It had only one door, no windows, and the kidnappers had secured that door somehow with bars."

Wanda sat transfixed, taking in the whole saga. "Wow!" she said. "That is amazing. You all were brilliant. I wish I'd been here."

"We felt like real detectives after they found those boys," said Tessa. "We could even be convinced that we saved their lives."

Olivia smiled. "Well, the thieves wanted only the bikes. They made sure the boys would be found and they never asked for ransom money or anything. The police said it was a very organized ring that works all over the southwest. Even so, it was exciting that we could figure out where the boys were so quickly."

"I think we should go into that business. We've read up on it with all the 'Ladies #1 Detective Agency' series," said Myra.

"I think that's the 'Number 1 Ladies' Detective Agency," corrected Kay.

"Whatever," said Myra. "I'm serious, though. We've had that dead body in the lake."

"What dead body?" asked Annabelle and Wanda at the same time.

"Oh, yes, you wouldn't have heard about that yet. Well, a couple of weeks or so ago they pulled a woman's body from Monte Verde Lake. We're waiting to hear about the toxicology reports. They don't know if it was an accident, suicide, or a murder," Tessa said.

"Oh my gosh," said Wanda. "I always thought Angel Fire was such a nice, quiet place."

Roberta smiled. "It really is, Wanda. Don't be alarmed."

The food came, and plates were passed to the appropriate person. "I'll bring some more coffee," said their server.

"But we do have a small police force," Myra continued their conversation. "I'm sure they could use our help. When we put our heads together, why, we can figure out anything."

Wanda chuckled her deep throaty laugh. "I'm liking this, ladies. First we need a name. How about 'Sweet Sleuths'?"

"Or 'Moreno Valley Snoop Sisters'," put in Tessa.

"Seriously," said Myra, "as soon as they release the toxicology info, we'll know what direction to consider. Besides, someone was saying the other day that it has hurt Wilda Acker's business at the RV Park. No one wants to stay there anymore. She's had cancelled reservations as well as fewer people who simply stop for a night or so. And you all know Wilda's situation. She needs that business in addition to her pension to make ends meet."

Kay looked at Roberta, hoping for reinforcement. "Let's wait until we see what the police or, I should say, the state troopers are doing, since they're the ones who investigate a death. There's a lot of other news to catch up on, like the situation with Bertie's son-in-law. We need to talk about our cookbook sales, and we want to hear how Mason is doing, Wanda."

"What about your son-in-law, Bertie?" asked Wanda.

Roberta sighed and shared with Wanda the background. "Mindy and the boys arrive tomorrow. They have all been working with a counselor, and Ted plans to come up every other weekend to see the kids. I don't know if I can stand to face him. I'm so angry with him for what he's done to the family."

Annabelle laid her hand on Roberta's arm. "I'm sure when the time comes you'll know how to act. I've come to the conclusion that, in the overall scheme of things, forgiveness is a gift to both parties."

"I know you're right," said Roberta. "I'm not quite ready for that yet, though."

"Tell us about Mason," Olivia said, turning toward Wanda.

"He's doing so well," she replied, her eyes shining with enthusiasm. "As his grandmother, I wish I could personally hug whoever discovered the therapeutic link between autistic kids and horseback riding. Mason loves it. The time he gets to go to the stables now is the highlight of his week." Here," she said picking up her iPhone. "I've got some recent pictures."

Roberta looked around at her group of friends as they passed around and admired the pictures Wanda shared. Wanda had seemed to carry some undercurrent of uneasiness, but it passed when she began talking about her grandson, Mason, so perhaps Roberta had been mistaken. Tuesday mornings together always brought a settled feeling when the group was all together, sharing, supporting, caring. In spite of the anguish she was feeling because of Ted's betrayal, at this moment in time Roberta had the sense of peace that being with close friends always brought. Even as she had that thought, Roberta knew that feeling would vanish with tomorrow's arrival of Mindy and the boys.

Tessa arrived home from the breakfast and was surprised to see Jim in the kitchen pouring a cup of coffee.

"I thought you'd be hard at work at your computer working on that new proposal you were telling me about," she said.

"I was working on it, but I needed a break. How was breakfast with the ladies?"

"Great, as usual. Both Annabelle and Wanda are back so we have a full circle again. That always feels good. We're all so proud of ourselves for figuring out where those mountain bikers were. Myra wants us to become detectives and help the police figure out about that woman who was in the lake."

"Oh, no. Please don't get involved with them in anything like that, Tess."

She smiled at her husband. "I make no promises."

He groaned. "Get yourself a cup of tea and let's sit together on the deck." He took his coffee and headed that direction.

Moments later Tessa joined him. They sat silently together for a while, lifting their faces to the warmth of the sunlight, relaxing in the fresh mountain air. A Broad-tailed Hummingbird darted by and hovered at the red geranium blossoms. A squirrel scolded them from a nearby ponderosa pine.

"How can the sky be so blue out here?" remarked Tessa. "I always want to describe it, but I can't. It's azure, or cerulean, or... what? I should ask Olivia what that color is called."

Jim squinted into the sun. He shrugged. "It's simply a New Mexico sky. That's all you need to say, isn't it?"

Tessa looked at her husband. "Jim, have you thought any more about being foster parents?"

Jim set down his coffee cup and, leaning toward her, took her hand in his. "Yes, I have. But what I've been wondering is why are you considering this? Do you wish we'd done more to try to have kids of our own? Do you feel like something's missing in our lives?" His thumb gently stroked her hand as he waited for her answer.

"Oh, not really. I love the work I do building websites for people. I love our life here, our friends and activities. I feel like we have a full life. It's only that, I don't know, sometimes I feel like there should be more. I should be doing something to pay back for all we have. I think about kids who live in bad circumstances. Children could thrive here. We could help that happen."

Jim let go of her hand and sat back, silent for a moment. "Then I think you should look into it," he finally said.

Tessa nodded and smiled. "Good. I will." She leaned back and closed her eyes. "Sometimes, though," she said very softly, "sometimes I do wish we had children of our own." She opened her eyes again and saw that Jim's expression had changed. His brow had furrowed and he had what she called "his worried face." She patted his hand. "But most of the time I'm simply grateful for the life we have." She sipped her tea and sighed a contented sigh.

Olivia arrived home and dropped her purse and car keys on the hall table. The house seemed so much quieter after having Tony and all the excitement of the weekend. Thinking about that made Olivia shake her head.

She still had trouble believing that her friends had figured out so quickly where the boys might be. She had been at the police headquarters that evening when Tessa had texted her with their suggestion about where to look. She would probably never tell them that the police had already come to the same conclusion after consulting maps showing any cabins in isolated areas, and they were already on their way to the boys.

Even so, she had to admit, that was pretty good detective work on their part. She wondered if they really would put their minds to solving the mystery surrounding the woman in the lake. *They probably will*, she thought. *I mean, WE probably will.* It felt good to be part of the Tuesday Breakfast Group. Olivia could hardly remember the time before she had started to join them for breakfast.

She moved on to her bedroom and pulled her painting shirt off the hook in the closet. As she changed her top, she gazed out toward the mountain. She thought back to her early years in Angel Fire, her sense of running away from her empty marriage, running to a place and time where she could feel fulfilled as an artist. Still, she had felt somewhat isolated and lonely until Roberta had suggested she join their group on Tuesday mornings. She smiled as she remembered her first thought, "Why would I want to be with those older women?"

That idea soon changed as she met them for breakfast a few times. She thought about how much they all had come to mean to her: Annabelle with her quiet wisdom; Wanda, whose enthusiasm and overflowing sense of joy lifted them up; Roberta, calm and caring; Kay, with her sense of style, spirituality, and basic optimism; Myra, with her casseroles –which revealed her loving heart in spite of her brusqueness; and Tessa, who had become her closest friend.

At first, Olivia had thought they were all comfortable women who didn't have a care in the world, but as she had gotten to know them she had come to realize that they all had heartaches or burdens, just as she did worrying about her mother's decline into dementia. *Yes,* she thought as she walked into her studio eager to begin painting, *there is something very special about the way women support and nurture each other.* She counted the Tuesday Breakfast Group among her blessings.

Myra had stopped at Lowe's on the way home to get the ingredients for a new cookie recipe she wanted to try, Swedish Almond Bars. She had signed up to make cookies for the church's fellowship time the next Sunday and she wanted to take something different.

As she was putting the supplies out on the counter, she glanced toward the locked door to the lower level apartment. She had known she would miss having Hannah and Shandra living down there, but she hadn't realized what an empty feeling their being gone would give her. Her own daughter, Amber, had thought Myra was foolish to let strangers stay there a whole year without charging any rent, but it had given Myra a wonderful feeling of satisfaction to be able to do that, even more than when she took an ill person a casserole. Hannah had been in such a dire situation, after all, having to live in their car. Anyway, it made Myra feel a little less lonely to have other people around.

She sighed and got to work on her new cookies. She always felt a little better when she was working in her kitchen, especially when she was cooking or baking for someone else.

Roberta and Kay laughed together on the way home, coming up with sillier and sillier names for their detective group; COPS for Cute Old People Sleuthing, and mottos like, "You do the crime- we find you in time."

"I bet Wanda could come up with a good tee shirt slogan for us," said Kay.

"She could," agreed Roberta as she stopped in Kay's driveway.

Before she got out, Kay turned to her friend. "I'll be thinking of you this week with the family arriving. If you ever need to get away, come on over. We'll have coffee."

"I will, thanks," said Roberta.

Kay started up her steps and Roberta backed out of the driveway and headed home.

When Kay opened the front door she had the strangest sense that something was not right. She glanced around the living room and started toward the kitchen. From where she stood she could see into the kitchen and her glance took in the opened jar of peanut butter on the counter, but her mind couldn't process why it would be there. She would never leave anything out on her counter like that. In that microsecond of time she realized someone had been in her house. She started to ease her way to the phone in the living room.

Suddenly, a strong arm wrapped around her, pinning her arms to her side while a hand slapped over her mouth. The smell of a sweaty body enveloped her.

"Don't," said a stranger's voice. "Don't you dare try to scream."

CHAPTER FIVE

K ay's heart sped out of control. She thought she might faint. Her knees buckled under her and she sagged against the intruder. She couldn't breathe. She struggled against the vise that was holding her.

"Lady, stop," said the voice behind her. "I'll let go if you won't scream, OK? You won't scream?"

Kay tried to nod, but he was holding her too tightly.

She felt his arms loosen her and she grabbed for the nearby end table to keep from falling. She turned slightly and collapsed on the couch, gasping for breath and trying to control the bile that rose in her throat. Her body trembled uncontrollably and tears poured from her eyes.

Finally, she dared to look at her captor. She gasped. She had expected a large man, but the person before her was a kid, a shaggy-haired, tattooed kid with a pimply face and a very tense expression.

"Lady, I'm sorry I scared you. I only broke in to get something to eat. I didn't think anyone would come in. I'm not going to hurt you. Honest."

It was a moment before Kay could speak. "You....Why?...Why did you come in here?"

He shrugged. "I dunno. It looked like a nice house. I peeked in the windows and no one was home. The door was unlocked."

Kay's heartrate was beginning to return to normal, but she couldn't stop shaking. "Are you a runaway?" She rubbed her arms, trying to bring herself under control.

The boy looked away and shifted his position as he stood in front of her. "Sorta."

"What do you mean, 'Sort of'?"

"I guess you're gonna turn me in, huh?" His shoulders slumped and he looked defeated.

"Well, you did break and enter my house. You grabbed me violently when I came in."

"Ah, I didn't mean to scare you. I just didn't want you to scream. I didn't think anyone would be around. I mean, it freaked me out when I heard you coming up the steps."

Kay took a deep breath. She stopped shivering and her fear turned to anger. "Well, what did you expect?" she exclaimed, raising her voice. "Did you think I simply would say 'Hello. What are you doing here?' Of course, I would scream! You scared me to death!"

"I'm sorry, Lady. I'm sorry. I was so hungry, though. I had to do something."

"Why were you so hungry? Where do you live? You'd better sit down and tell me the whole story or I'll call the police immediately. And you'd better tell me the truth." Kay's teacher voice had come back automatically, and the boy promptly sat in the chair opposite Kay.

"All right," she said. "Start from the beginning."

After a deep sigh, the teenager began. "OK, here's what happened. I ran away from home six months ago, and,"

"Where was 'home'?" she asked.

"Albuquerque. I lived there with my mom and her boyfriend. I finally got tired of his beating me for every little thing, or just for fun when he was drunk. She never did nothin' to stop him. So I ran away." He stopped and looked at Kay.

"What's your name?" she asked.

"Jeremy."

"Jeremy what?"

"Jeremy Townson."

"So, then what happened, Jeremy?"

He squirmed slightly in the chair. "Well, I went to Santa Fe. Knew a guy there and I crashed with him, but then he left town so I hung out with some homeless guys for a while."

"Wasn't your mom looking for you?"

"Nah, probably not. I think she's glad I'm gone."

"So, how did you get here, to Angel Fire?"

He shrugged and looked away.

"Jeremy, I want the truth."

"OK," he muttered. "I got caught stealing some stuff from a convenience store in Santa Fe. They took me to Juvie Hall. It's kinda lax there, and one day I slipped away while they were takin' some of us to talk to some counselor or somethin'."

"And you came up here? How long ago was that?"

"Well, first I hitchhiked to Taos. It's easy to get lost around Taos. Nobody notices you there. I guess I'd been there about two months. I only came up here a few weeks ago, to try someplace different, you know?"

Kay didn't know, couldn't imagine what this boy's life had been like. "I think that before I call the police, I want you to talk to our minister, Richard Safford. He understands kids. Maybe he could help you get your life straightened out." *Am I really saying that to this intruder, this kid who broke into my home and who almost suffocated me a few minutes ago? What am I thinking?*

Jeremy put up both hands as if backing away. "No way. I ain't gonna talk to no preacher."

Kay stopped herself from saying "Two negatives make an affirmative", but instead she said, "Don't say 'ain't'."

"Well, I'm not."

"Look, you're in a pretty bad place, Jeremy. First, you're a runaway; second, you're a fugitive; and last, you're homeless and starving. Don't you think it's time to get some help?"

Jeremy looked at Kay directly and shook his head. "And why would you help me?"

Kay almost smiled. "That's a good question, and I'm not sure myself. I guess it's because I like to think I'm a Christian, and an important question is 'what would Jesus do', and...."

Jeremy scoffed. "Jesus, ha. Who believes that stuff?"

Kay sat back. "I do. If I didn't, I already would have called 911 and said 'good riddance' to you."

"How do you know I'm telling the truth? Maybe I'm just blowin' smoke....I mean, maybe I'm full of...stuff."

"That's possible. Are you?"

A slight smile came to Jeremy's lips. "Are you for real, Lady?"

"My name is Mrs. Tucker. Yes, I'm for real, and it seems to me that you're someone who needs a second chance. I'm a great believer in second chances."

Saturday, Roberta picked up Kay to take their turn selling cookbooks at Lowe's. They were setting up the table when Myra hurried in.

"I just met a reporter from the Albuquerque Journal who is up here following a story. You'll never guess! That woman found in the lake? They are looking at it as a possible homicide. She may have been murdered!" Myra wore the smug expression of someone who was first with the news.

"Murdered!" both Kay and Roberta exclaimed at the same time. "What do they think happened?" Kay added.

"They said there had been a sharp blow to the head, but the water in her lungs showed that drowning was the cause of death. There are no suspects and no motive yet. They say it may still turn out to be an accident or even a suicide, but they are considering homicide."

"Oh, the poor thing," said Roberta.

"You know what this means, don't you?" said Myra.

"What?"

"It means the state police need our help. There aren't any clues, I guess, so we have to figure out what happened."

"Myra, for heaven's sake!" exclaimed Kay. "There is no way a bunch of women are going to solve a murder."

"And why not? We were so fast at thinking where those mountain bikers were, weren't we? And last year, remember? I deduced that Hannah and Shandra were living in their car. We're naturals. We just have to put our heads together and we can figure out who did this terrible thing."

Roberta turned away to engage a tourist in conversation and sold her a cookbook. When she finished she smiled at Myra. "Let's remember why we're here at Lowe's today and sell some of these cookbooks so we can send Shandra book money for college."

"Of course," Myra said, nodding enthusiastically. "I'll see you both at breakfast Tuesday and, in the meantime, I'll try to learn some more details. We can talk about it then." Myra swished her way through the sliding doors into Lowe's.

"I'll bet she's getting some casserole ingredients," muttered Kay.

Roberta tried to hide her grin. "Now, be nice, Kay."

Kay had already moved a short distance away with a cookbook in hand to greet a fellow Bridge player.

The morning flew by as the two women greeted friends, acquaintances, and tourists and explained their cookbook mission. To their delight they had sold quite a few by the time Tessa and Olivia came at noon to relieve them.

Kay brought the newcomers up to date on what they had done that morning, and then added, "Myra came by with the report that the woman in the lake might actually have been murdered. She thinks we can solve the murder. Honestly!"

"But what a neat idea," said Olivia. "I love puzzles, murder mysteries and things."

"Sure, but this is a real murder, or at least it might be, and it's someone we don't know. We know nothing about her at all," Kay reminded Olivia.

"Neither do detectives when they begin an investigation," said Tessa. "I think it will be fun."

Roberta gathered up her purse and took out her car keys. "Well, I guess that means we'd better be thinking up a name for ourselves."

Roberta and Kay started the drive up the hill towards Kay's house. "So, how are Mindy and the boys?" asked Kay.

Roberta sighed. "It broke my heart when they first arrived. They all seemed so...so fragile or something. It was like none of us knew quite how to act, what to say. Things are a little better now. We've sort of fallen into a routine. Al is giving the boys lots of attention. They'll start golf camp on Monday and they're excited about that."

"And Mindy?"

"Mindy is devastated. What Ted did has put them all in jeopardy because of the finances. He'll be up here next weekend to see the boys, and I dread seeing him myself. I want to slap him silly!"

"Of course, you do. I would, too. You mentioned one time that they were getting counseling. Do you think it will help?"

"I hope so. Mindy thinks that at the very least it will help her and the boys sort through their feelings. Ted has some redeeming traits. He has been a wonderful father. The boys adore him and Mindy, my dear, foolish daughter, says she still loves him. But, they cannot remain a family unless he stops gambling. He is trying to, Mindy says, but I don't know if a person can stop an addiction like that." Tears had burned her eyes as she shared her concerns with Kay. She blinked them back.

"I, too, am praying that he can get it under control," said Kay as they pulled into her driveway. "I was saying to someone recently that I'm a person who believes in second chances. I think Jesus' example taught us to believe in them, don't you? I hope that Ted can make good use of a second chance to pull his family together again. Sometimes people can end up stronger after something like this."

"I hope you're right. Mindy is even hopeful that by the end of the summer they can go back to Albuquerque and start fresh." Roberta smiled at her friend as Kay got her keys out of her purse.

"Are you locking your house these days, Kay?" she asked.

"Oh, well, I started to, recently. Something on TV made me think of it. I forget exactly what, but something I saw made me think it's a good idea."

"Angel Fire has always been such a safe place. We don't think about locking during the day when we're in and out, but I guess it's probably a good idea."

"I guess so. Anyway, I'll see you Tuesday, Sister Sleuth."

Roberta chuckled and waved goodbye.

Kay let herself in her house and quickly turned off the alarm system. She and her husband had installed the system many years before, but they never actually used it. Now, Kay used it constantly.

She went to the locked door from the kitchen to the garage and opened it.

"Are you here, Jeremy?" she called.

Jeremy Townson slipped out from behind a shelter Kay had helped him arrange for himself in the back corner of the garage. "Yeah, I'm here."

"You can come inside for a little while if you want to." Kay said, holding the door wider open.

Jeremy shuffled sullenly past her. Kay shook her head and followed him into the kitchen. "There's some milk in the refrigerator, and some cereal in the cabinet. Fix yourself some breakfast."

"Can I eat watching the TV?"

"No, Jeremy, you can't. Besides, I want to talk to you. You can't simply hang out here in my garage. You need to be thinking of your future."

"I ain't got no future," he growled under his breath. He got the cereal from the cupboard and went to the refrigerator for the milk.

"Of course, you have a future. You're a young man. Clean yourself up and stop your bad attitude. Get a job and become self-sufficient."

"Easy for you to say." He got a bowl down from the shelf and poured a liberal amount of cereal in it. "Sure, you're bein' nice to me, but you don't trust me for a minute. I have to stay in the garage. You keep all the doors locked and set your alarm when you're going out and at night. Why? Do you think I'll come rob or murder you in the night or something?" He plopped down at the kitchen table and began eating.

Kay sat down across from him. "I don't think you would, but how could I really know what you'll do? I don't know you, Jeremy. If my family or friends knew you were here they'd call the police immediately. All day when I am home you're welcome in the house to eat meals, use the bathroom, even watch TV. That's being very generous of me, I think. I've offered to have you talk to Richard Safford, our minister, but you refuse. I know he could help you figure out what to do. Of course, you're free to leave any time you want. There's a door from the garage to the outside. You can open it and go if you choose to."

Jeremy looked up from his breakfast, and Kay was struck with how gaunt the boy looked. He paused, as if choosing his words carefully for the first time. "Could I stay here for a little while? I got so darn tired out there, grubbing for something to eat, worrying about where to sleep. I feel like I need to take a deep breath and kinda catch up with myself, you know?"

"All right. I'll give you this week here. Next Saturday is the hot air balloon festival. You might enjoy that. They'll be a large crowd so you won't be noticed. After that, let's make a plan, OK?"

Jeremy nodded and went back to shoveling the cereal into his mouth.

CHAPTER SIX

Tuesday morning was overcast when the Breakfast Group met at The Bakery. No one complained about that, though, because as long as it stayed cool, the group enjoyed the climate of Angel Fire. Everyone had people back in Texas or Oklahoma who were reporting the sweltering temperatures. Besides, they knew it would soon clear off and the bright New Mexico sun would find its rightful place in the sky. Stan Samuels always gave them a big welcome when they had breakfast at The Bakery, and that added to their good spirits.

The group of friends gathered with the usual greetings. Roberta had brought Mindy, and everyone greeted her warmly, noting and understanding the sadness she seemed to carry with her. Wanda's tee shirt said "iTired There's a nap for that." Myra looked like she was bursting with news, but as soon as they had placed their orders, Roberta began reporting on the cookbook sales.

"So, shall we keep selling through July, and then send the money to Shandra so she has it when school starts to help with her book expenses?" Roberta looked around the group for a consensus and easily got it.

"Now," began Myra, leaning forward in her excitement, "let's look at the mystery here in Angel Fire."

In her eagerness to begin she didn't notice Kay rolling her eyes so she went right on.

"These are the facts so far. I got them from the newspaper." She pulled a legal pad from her large purse and looked at her notes. "Beverly Tensley was pulled from Monte Verde Lake the afternoon of May 5th, 2015. She had no identification on her, but the police had known that a woman hadn't returned to her cabin at the Bobcat Meadows RV/Cabins Park since April 17th."

"How did they know that?" asked Tessa.

"Well, Wilda told me. She plays Bridge with the wife of one of the policemen, you know Felicia Landry, don't you? Anyway, Wilda was mentioning to Felicia that she didn't know if the woman had skipped town or what, and wondered if she should report her as a missing person, so she was asking Felicia what she thought."

Wanda asked, "Do you think she was in the lake all that time? Wouldn't she have decomposed or something?"

Annabelle shuddered at the image.

"I looked into that," said Myra. "I googled it and learned that if the body is in cold water, it could last for several weeks. What happens, though, is that they get bloated from gas inside them and rise to the surface. That's why someone saw the body when they were walking their dog."

"Myra!" exclaimed Kay just as the server brought their food, "we're going to be eating. Please wait until later to give us all these gory details."

"Sorry, but these are the facts. Detectives aren't supposed to let those things bother them."

"Well, we're not detectives, and those things do bother me, so please wait until after breakfast to tell us." Kay picked up her fork to dive into her scrambled eggs and scowled at Myra.

Annabelle looked around the table. "I'm sure we're all interested, Myra, but let's use this time for our usual topics of books and local news." She gave Myra one of her warm smiles, and Myra shrugged and put away her pad.

Mindy whispered to her mom, "You all have changed since I was here last," and Roberta simply winked at her.

"I am reading a wonderful book," continued Annabelle. "It's called 'Voice of a Voyage' by Doann Houghton-Alico. It is so beautifully written and it really makes you think."

Wanda looked up with interest. "What's it about?"

"It's a travel memoir," Annabelle replied. "The author and her husband took ten years sailing around the world in their sailboat. They started when the author was sixty. She's also a poet, and the book includes some of her poetry. Really, it's fascinating, and so well written."

The group slipped back into their routine of sharing tidbits of this and that. The upcoming balloon festival was a big topic. As they talked about it, Kay remembered her words to Jeremy. That would be an important day as he would have to decide what he was going to do. *Should I tell my friends about Jeremy? No, they wouldn't understand, but there's something about that young man that makes me believe he can get straightened out.* It was increasingly difficult for her to keep Jeremy's existence to herself, however, especially with Roberta. It was rare for them not to confide in each other. Kay found it a little easier to keep this secret since Roberta was so preoccupied with Mindy and the boys and their situation but, even so, she was uncomfortable about it.

Myra set down her coffee cup and turned to Kay. "Have you seen any more of that handsome retired minister?"

"Actually, although it's not really your business, we did run into each other at the library one day and went to lunch together. He's a nice man."

"He was on the last trekkers hike Jim and I did," said Tessa. "He has a good sense of humor. He told several funny stories about his work in the ministry."

"I think ministers must need a sense of humor to get through all they have to do," commented Annabelle. The group nodded.

"All right, we're all finished." Myra brought out the pad and a pen again. "Let's get to work, ladies."

"Are you serious about this, Myra? How do you think we could possibly figure out what happened to that poor woman?" asked Roberta.

"Bertie, don't be so pessimistic. If we all put our heads together we can come up with the solution. It's because we're all so different and so we bring different aspects to the questions. We only need to let our imaginations go to work."

"Well, that's never been a problem for this group," said Tessa. "I'm game. What will it hurt if we try?"

Myra looked around at each one, nodded and began again. "I talked to Wilda to see what she knew about this woman, Beverly."

"Yes, I think we should always call her by name. It will make it more personal; then we'll care more about her," said Wanda.

"Right. In fact, Wilda called her 'Bev' so let's call her that. Although all Wilda knew about her was that she had come from Albuquerque, was divorced, and had worked most recently as a dealer in a casino. Bev was very physically fit, hiked a lot, and gathered native things like mushrooms and dandelions and used them in cooking."

"So," said Olivia, leaning forward, "since she was physically fit she should have been able to fight off an attacker, at least for a little while. Were there any signs of an attack on her?"

Myra shrugged. "I don't know."

"And no one at the RV park mentioned hearing a commotion, right?" asked Roberta, feeling herself warm to the project.

"There hasn't been anything about that, and Wilda didn't say anything about it so I guess not."

Annabelle drummed her fingers on the table as she sat thinking. "What that says to me is that if it was a murder, she probably knew her murderer, and even more, she must have trusted him. It could have been a relative or a friend."

"Right," said Kay, enthusiastically in spite of herself. "I'm sure the state trooper is interviewing all those people."

"But what family does she have? Didn't it take a while for the police to locate her family? Did Wilda say anything about friends coming to see her?" Olivia said.

Myra was jotting notes on her pad. "I'll check out these questions and let you know next Tuesday."

"Are you going to talk to the state trooper who is the investigator?" asked Wanda.

"I think I'll talk to Wilda first. She can probably answer most of these questions. She's pretty anxious to get this resolved since it is hurting her business. She said that there's that yellow police tape around the cabin now. Ever since they put that up people have been checking out of the RV park."

Tessa's head jerked up. "I just thought of something. Remember that the mountain bike thieves locked those boys up on Baldy? Well, that RV park is almost opposite Baldy, isn't it? Maybe this Bev saw something suspicious while she was out hiking or gathering berries or something. Maybe the bike thieves caught her snooping around and decided to kill her to keep her quiet."

The friends looked at each other, alarm showing in their expressions.

"But that doesn't make sense, though," said Annabelle after a moment's thought. "For one thing, they were up there after she was murdered, and for another, the robbers gave that clue so the boys would be found. They didn't want a death on their hands, it seems."

"Maybe they didn't want the boys killed because they didn't want ANOTHER murder on their hands," Olivia said.

Myra was rapidly jotting notes. "At this point, we can't discount anything." She stopped writing and looked up. "OK, I think this is enough to get us started. Keep thinking and we'll work on it again next week. I'll let the state trooper who is in charge know about the mountain bike thieves." She smiled at everyone. "Good work, team."

Kay almost groaned out loud.

When Kay got home she let Jeremy into the house. "Jeremy, it's not good for a young man your age to simply hang around the house all the time. Do you want to go hiking or anything?"

Jeremy looked at her as if she suggested he climb Mt. Everest. "Hiking? No way."

"Well, what about reading? I could get you some books from the library."

"I don't read so good."

Kay tried not to let her exasperation show. "Well, what do you like to do?"

Jeremy shrugged. "Nothin, really. I like to watch TV. I like to do games."

"Games?" Kay brightened at the idea. "I've got lots of games for the grandkids, Monopoly, Scrabble,"

"Not those games," he scoffed. "You know, electronic games. But I'm sure you don't got any of those, do you?"

"No. My family always brings their own iPads or whatever. Oh, well. I tried, anyway. You might as well get yourself some breakfast if you want." Kay walked away to hide her annoyance. *This boy sure makes being a Christian a hard job!*

Later that day, Mindy joined her mother in the kitchen to help prepare lunch. "Mom, you know what gave me the creeps this morning when Myra was talking about the murder?"

"What's that, hon?" Roberta brought the luncheon meat and cheese to the counter as Mindy got out the bread.

"When she gave the date that woman went missing, April 17th, remember?"

Her mother nodded.

"We were here then. That was our last visit. I thought I remembered that as the time we all were here so I checked when we got back. Not only were we here then, but that was the evening that Ted went for that drive by himself."

Roberta stopped setting out the sandwich things and stared at Mindy. "What are you saying? You don't think..." It was impossible for her to finish the sentence.

"Oh, no. No, Mom. I didn't mean that at all. Ted couldn't, wouldn't ever hurt someone like that. I only meant, maybe he saw something without realizing that it was connected to the death. When he gets up here this weekend I'll ask him about it. I know he loves to go to the lake. He says the calm water helps him think when he's trying to figure out a problem with work or something. Wouldn't that be something if he saw anything suspicious there?"

"That is creepy, Mindy. Don't tell Myra if you see her around town. She won't stop nagging you to find out."

Mindy smiled. "Don't worry. I know I always need to watch what I say around Myra."

"Myra has a good heart. She thinks everyone's business is hers because she's interested in everyone. It can make for some misunderstandings sometimes, though."

Scott and Walker burst into the kitchen. "Is lunch ready yet?" asked Scott.

"Yeah, we're hungry," added Walker.

Roberta looked at her two grandsons and marveled at how much they brightened up a room with their very presence.

Kay walked through the living room on her way from her room to the kitchen. Jeremy was hunkered down on the couch staring at some reality show rerun on the TV. As she passed him, he looked up. "Mrs. Tucker, can I ask you something?"

She paused and smiled at him. "Of course." Every time she looked at Jeremy she saw behind his tough-guy, aloof exterior and saw the vulnerable boy hidden inside. She had seen many kids like that throughout her years of teaching and, as always, her heart went out to him.

"I just don't get it. I mean, I can't understand. Why're you bein' so nice to me? I ain't done nothin' for you."

Kay walked around and sat by him on the couch. "It's hard to explain, Jeremy, but it's because of grace," she began.

"Who's Grace?"

Kay had to chuckle. "Not a who, a what. Grace is something we, as Christians, have come to understand through the way Jesus lived. It means that God loves us even when we don't deserve it. Because of that we, in turn, are supposed to love and care for other people even if they don't do anything to earn it. When I first saw you, I could see that you were someone who hadn't experienced that. I don't know. As I said, it's hard to explain, but I felt like God was giving me an opportunity to help you experience grace. Do you see?"

"No, I don't get it at all, but that don't mean I'm not glad to be here. I...I guess I haven't shown that. Maybe I could do somethin' around here to help you, you know? Some chore or somethin'."

Kay thought a minute. "Well, you could sweep the deck for me."

Jeremy clicked off the TV. "OK. Where's a broom?"

CHAPTER SEVEN

Kay was taking a load out of the dryer when her doorbell rang. She glanced at the deck where Jeremy had finished sweeping and was now washing down her porch furniture, then scurried to the door.

Seeing Ben there with his arms full, she opened the door. "Hello, Ben. What in the world...?"

"I was driving by a roadside stand and they had the most wonderful peaches and melons from Colorado. I guess I went a little wild buying them so I decided to share them with you. Can I come in?"

"Oh, of course." Kay looked anxiously toward the deck. "Here, let me take those things. I'll just put them in the kitchen and...."

"No, I'll drop everything if I try to hand it to you. Which way is the kitchen? Oh, I see it straight ahead." He moved past her and carried the load into the kitchen, setting everything down on the table. He looked up and smiled at her. He glanced around. "What a nice, sunny kitchen, and with a deck, too." He glimpsed Jeremy working on the furniture. "Is that your grandson?"

Kay felt a few nervous butterflies in her stomach. She wondered how much to tell him. *He's a minister, after all. He should understand.* In that moment, she decided to share the whole story with him.

"No, he's not my grandson. I actually didn't even know him until recently. He's a young man in a very bad situation and he needs some help. Could I fix you a cup of coffee and tell you about him?"

Ben looked momentarily confused, but nodded and accepted her offer. While Kay got the coffeepot going and brought out mugs, she thanked him for the bountiful produce he'd brought. She glanced to the deck and saw that Jeremy had realized she had company, and he had slipped away down the deck steps into the yard and was probably hiding out in the garage.

"Do you take cream or sugar?" she asked.

"Just black, thanks." He sat at the table and reached for the mug she handed him. The aroma of freshly brewed coffee swirled around them along with Kay's feelings of uncertainty. She thought she could trust Ben with her secret, but what if she was wrong?

Once they were seated across from each other, Kay sighed, trying to decide where to begin. She looked into the kind blue eyes of her new friend and started at the beginning. "When I got home from breakfast one morning, Jeremy was here, in my house. I always left the house unlocked during the day. He had been homeless for a while, a runaway, then in trouble for stealing food in Santa Fe. He was so hungry that he came in looking for food when no one was home. I surprised him when I came in."

She paused and looked at Ben to see how he was reacting to the story. She saw only understanding in his expression, so she continued. "I saw a boy who has had such a bad start in life. He told me that his mother's boyfriend would get drunk and beat him, and he thinks his mother is glad he left. He feels that he has no future."

"And so, you took him in?" asked Ben. He had set his mug on the table and was leaning forward, listening carefully.

"Well, not exactly. I mean, I didn't know him at all. I fixed a sleeping place for him in the garage, and when I'm not here or at night when I go to bed, I lock the door from the garage to the house and I put the alarm on. But when I'm home, he stays in the house."

"And you fix him his meals?"

"Yes. He was so hungry, so thin. He'd run away from juvenile hall in Santa Fe and was hanging out with some people in Taos, then came up here a month or so ago."

Ben smiled at her and shook his head. "Does anyone else know he's here?"

"No. I was afraid to say anything, even to my friends, even Bertie, and I couldn't tell my children. If I told anyone, I was afraid they would make me turn him in."

"How long did you think you could go on like this, Kay? After all, the boy is a fugitive."

"I know. I know." Kay looked at her hands in her lap. She was surprised to feel tears burning her eyes. "I only wanted to give him a chance. I don't think he's ever had a lucky break in his life. I did tell him that Saturday after the balloon festival, we would have to make a plan."

Ben sat silent for a moment. He took a sip of coffee, and then set the mug down again. "Let me talk to the boy, Kay. Maybe I can help. Before I was a minister, I was an attorney for a few years. I know a little bit about the system. If he didn't have any record before, I might be able to arrange for community service. They've done that in Cimarron, I know. A lot depends on him, on his attitude."

Kay grimaced slightly. "He doesn't have the best attitude, I'm afraid. It's because he's afraid to trust people, to believe in good things. It breaks my heart to see the wall he's put around himself."

"Yes, of course. But, Kay, his being here is not a good situation for you, a woman alone. I have an extra bedroom. I've worked with kids all my adult life. What do you think about my keeping him while we work out some plan for him?"

"But, you haven't even met him."

Ben shrugged. "Let me meet him and talk to him. Then let's see what we should do."

Kay sat wordlessly for a moment. She had forgotten the comforting feeling of having someone to shoulder a burden, to solve a problem, to be a partner. Yet, here was this person she hardly knew who was willing to take on this challenge. She bit her lower lip to keep from blurting out words that might embarrass her.

Finally, she was able to whisper, "I don't know what to say."

"I may be retired from serving a church, Kay, but I hope I never retire from serving a loving Lord. There is a need here, and perhaps I can help. What's the boy's name?"

"Jeremy Townson."

"Call Jeremy in, and let's see what happens." Ben leaned back and lifted his mug for another sip.

Kay got up and went to the garage door. Opening it, she called Jeremy. As he walked past her into the kitchen, his eyes were full of fear.

The upcoming weekend carried the promise of good things, beautiful weather and the much-anticipated hot air balloon festival. However, for several of the JULIETs it also carried uncertainty and uneasy feelings; Roberta would have to face her son-in-law; Kay would learn what Ben had resolved with Jeremy; Tessa would sit down with Jim to fill out the application for being foster parents and, on Friday, Wanda would learn the results of some medical tests she had not yet dared to mention even to her friends.

After lunch Al joined Roberta on the deck where she was watering the flowers.

"These petunias, geraniums, and marigolds smell so good," Roberta commented as she plucked off the dead blooms. "We get lots of hummingbirds without even putting out a hummingbird feeder."

Al leaned back in the cushioned deck chair. "Will we actually have to see Ted?" he asked.

After a pause, Roberta said, "I certainly hope not. He'll be staying at the resort and Mindy will take the boys over to him. I guess he'll be the one bringing them back here, but maybe he'll drop them off out front." She came and sat by her husband. "I'm afraid of what I might say if I see him. I am so furious at what he's done."

"Me, too. Mindy seems to be the one who is handling this best. She's hopeful they will work things out."

"Of course, that would be the best possible solution, so I'm hoping for that also. But the thing is," she sighed, "The thing is, how can you ever trust someone again after they have betrayed you? And, if you never can really believe in them, what kind of marriage is that?"

Al sat quietly for a moment or two, lost in thought. "We've been lucky, you and me, Bertie. We've been damn lucky."

"Is that what makes a good marriage? Luck?"

He leaned forward and patted her hand. "No, but it sure helps. What makes a good marriage is believing in the marriage enough to work at keeping it going in those times when you don't love your partner enough. That's what Mindy's doing now, I think."

"And I guess what we're supposed to do is simply be there for Mindy and the boys while they go through this."

"That's about it, Bertie. This is a good place for kids to be. I have to admit, I love having those boys around, although they do wear me out. We'd better be sure we take extra vitamins, old girl."

Roberta stood and went back to the flowers. "Be careful who you're calling 'old'. Don't forget, I'm five years younger than you."

Al sat quietly with his eyes closed while Roberta finished up with the flowers. She returned to her seat next to him, brushing off some potting soil from her hands as she sat down.

"Mindy told me something interesting this week. It's about that woman who was found in the lake."

Al's eyes opened, and he waited to hear more.

"We were talking about it at breakfast Tuesday. You know, Myra wants us to figure out what happened."

"What? Bertie, don't you get mixed up in all that. In the first place, it's none of your business, and in the second place, it could be dangerous. It might have been a murder, after all."

"Oh, don't worry. It's only for fun. We're not really getting involved, only seeing if we can figure out what happened."

"Well, I don't think it's a good idea. That Myra could lead you all into a world of trouble."

"Al, for heaven's sake! Do you want to know what Mindy said or not?"

"Yes, of course. What did she say?"

"They were here then. That was when they came up for a few days in April, remember? Not only that, but the woman apparently died around the time Ted went off by himself that evening. When Mindy told me that, I thought she was saying that maybe Ted was involved in whatever happened to that woman, but…."

"What? Ted might be a murderer?"

"No, let me finish. That was what I first thought she was saying, and I was as shocked as you, but that's not what she meant. She said that Ted liked to go to the lake so maybe he saw something suspicious, that's all. But wouldn't that be something if he had some evidence?"

Al shook his head. "You've been spending too much time with Myra."

Roberta squinted her eyes and gave Al a fierce look. "Are you trying to tell me who to be friends with? Is this one of the times when a person needs to believe in the marriage because she's mad at her husband?"

Al laughed, leaned over, and kissed Roberta's cheek. "Whatever works, my love. Whatever works."

Tessa and Jim sat at their kitchen table, a bowl of grapes in the center and each with a glass of herbal iced tea.

"So, what have we got to do?" asked Jim.

Tessa spread out the papers she had brought to the table. "Let's see. I filled out the first inquiry form and emailed it in. They sent this packet of stuff, information about the program, frequently asked questions, and the actual application form."

"Well, my first question is what do they require of us?"

Tessa smiled at her husband and shuffled through the papers. "I've got that right here. OK. Here are the requirements: you have to be eighteen or over; healthy; pass a fingerprint criminal record check; be a New Mexico resident; willing to attend 32 hours free training; willing to participate in a free home study; be committed to caring for children; and single or married. We're qualified on all those things."

"Are they going to try to pressure us to adopt the child, do you think?"

"I don't think so, hon, because they emphasize that the first goal is to have the original family get back together."

Jim nodded. "That's good. The other side of that, though, is how hard is it to part with a child you've had for a while and come to love, then they go back home?"

"Yes, that would be part of it. I guess there's a fine line between caring and caring too much. Here's something they say in this material. 'Foster parents open their homes and their hearts to children in custody by allowing them to feel safe, grow and learn in a family setting. Foster parents encourage children in their home to remain connected to their religion, culture and community. Foster parents can be part of a child's life even after they have returned home, if they choose to and the child and family are willing.' What do you think, Jim? Is this something we could do?"

Jim sat back, obviously in deep thought. After a moment he leaned forward. "Here's what I think. If we do this, we're opening ourselves up to a much more complicated life. I think we could handle that part. It's the emotional roller-coaster I'm worried about. Honestly, Tess, I think you have so much love to give a child in need that it would be a wonderful thing to do this. But, at the other end of having a foster child, when they go back home, I think that could be so hard for you, for both of us. So, I don't know. I really don't. I think we need to think about this for a while."

"I have been thinking about it for quite a while. I can understand your hesitancy. I know it would be hard to see a child go after we have invested a lot in them, but isn't the risk worth it, Jim, for the sake of the child? I didn't need to go into foster care, thank God, but I grew up in a home that was lacking in love and nurturing for us kids. I hate to think about kids who are in homes that are unsafe for them, or where they don't get the nurturing that kids need to become successful adults. I'm willing to take the risk to give a child that. I'm willing, Jim. Are you?"

CHAPTER EIGHT

Roberta pulled on her lightweight jacket as she and Al went out the door on their way to the balloon festival. Earlier, the boys had scurried to their dad's car the minute he drove in the driveway to pick them up. Mindy had opted to sleep in. Daylight had barely settled over the valley, but the day promised to be bright and sunny as the dawn announced itself in a rosy, golden exclamation.

"Are we supposed to pick up Kay on the way?" asked Al.

"No. I was surprised that she didn't want us to. She said she'd meet us there."

As they approached the balloon lift-off area, cars lined the sides of Mountain View Boulevard and spilled into the parking lot. Hundreds of people milled around as the giant balloons were unpacked and made ready to fill with hot air. An electricity of expectation surrounded the area as flames whooshed out and balloons unfurled.

Roberta caught a glimpse of Kay and Ben with a teenaged boy. Whispering to Al, she said, "No wonder Kay didn't want us to pick her up. She's over there with Ben and some boy. It must be one of his grandkids. Let's go say hello."

As they made their way through the crowd Al looked around and said, "I'm sure we'll see Ted and the boys. What do we do?"

"Well, we can't ignore our grandsons if they come up to us. We'll just have to be cordial, that's all."

"Even if it kills us," muttered Al, but he put a smile on his face as they joined Ben, Kay and the boy.

Greeting one another, Ben said, "And this is Jeremy."

"Oh, is he your grandson?" asked Roberta. She noticed that Kay seemed uncomfortable, but Ben answered with ease, "No, he's a special friend."

What is this all about? she wondered. She smiled at Jeremy. "And where do you live?" she asked.

Jeremy glanced at Kay then at Ben. "I, uh…"

"He's staying with me for a little while," Ben answered for him.

"Look," said Kay, pointing toward the balloons. "They're starting to fill them up. It won't be long until the lift off." The group began to move toward the launch site. The crews surrounding each balloon worked calmly and quietly, some keeping the ropes connected to the tops of the balloons taut, some holding the baskets in place, some firing up the flames through the fans to bring the balloons to their full glory. It was the spectators milling around who sparkled with anticipation.

Tessa and Olivia called to them from the crowd and slipped through to join them.

"Annabelle set up a card table to sell the rest of the cookbooks, and she's almost sold out. That was such a good idea to raise money for Shandra," said Olivia.

"Great," said Roberta. "We can get a check off to her soon, then."

"Where's Jim?" asked Al.

"He said that if he had to get up this early he was going fishing," replied Tessa. She laughed. "He has become quite the fly fisherman."

"We have the streams for it all around here," said Al.

"I haven't gone fly fishing in years," said Ben. "I'd sure like to get back to that."

"Jim would love to take you anytime. You might start out getting Jason Sides to go. He is a Fishing Guide, and knows all the best places. You could take your grandson," Tessa said, nodding at Jeremy who was starting to melt away in the mass of people.

"He's not my grandson, just a special friend. But he'll be staying with me for a while and I'd love to introduce him to fishing. Thanks for the information."

As one by one the colorful hot air balloons grew larger and began lifting off the ground, there were smatterings of applause and oohs and ahs from the spectators. Tessa took Kay's and Roberta's arms and, moving them a few steps away from the men she whispered, "Olivia and I did some investigating on Facebook. We found out some very interesting things about our victim."

"Great. What did you find?" Both Roberta's and Kay's expression showed their eagerness to hear more.

"It can wait until Tuesday, but let's simply say our victim isn't quite the nice, sweet lady that we thought she was," said Olivia.

"That's not fair. You get our interest, and then you leave us hanging," moaned Kay.

Grinning, Tessa said, "Sorry, but this isn't the time or the place to go into details."

Ben ambled over to the women. "Do you see Jeremy?" he asked.

The women glanced round, their eyes skimming the many people. "There he is," said Kay, pointing to Jeremy. He was talking to a group of four or five very tough-looking young men. He was shaking his head 'no', as if in an argument of some kind. One of the young men grabbed his arm as Jeremy started to turn away.

Ben was quickly by his side. "Anything wrong?"

The young man dropped his grasp on Jeremy's arm. "No. Not a thing." He and his friends turned and moved away.

"Are they friends of yours, Jeremy?" asked Ben.

"No way! I knew them when I was stayin' in Taos, is all. I didn't need you to come rescue me, ya know."

Ben put his hand on Jeremy's shoulder as they walked back toward the balloon launch. "I may not have needed to, but I wanted to, son. As long as I'm responsible for you, I intend to look out for you."

Even though Jeremy muttered it under his breath, Ben could clearly hear his comment. "I ain't your son, and no one's responsible for me."

As they approached the others, Ben uttered a silent prayer. *Lord, this boy is hurting badly. Give me the patience to deal with him and the wisdom to help him.* Ben and Kay communicated with a look that said a lot, and it didn't go without Roberta's noticing.

Wanda and her husband, Robert, joined the group. "Aren't they beautiful?" exclaimed Wanda. Everyone was squinting into the rising sunlight as the many-hued balloons climbed higher in the morning sky.

"Wanda, how come you're wearing a tee shirt without any great wisdom on it?" asked Olivia.

Wanda shrugged. "I didn't feel like it today, I guess." Her friends noticed that her smile carried a trace of wistfulness.

"Is anything wrong?" asked Roberta.

Wanda answered without looking directly at her. "I hope not. We can talk about it Tuesday, OK?"

Roberta paused, a concerned look on her face. "Sure. OK." *Looks like our Tuesday breakfast is going to be a full morning,* she thought.

The chase trucks headed out as the balloons spread out across the sky. The reds, yellows, and blues shimmered in the sunlight, their baskets becoming smaller and smaller. The clusters of spectators stayed grouped around, eyes to the sky, wanting the happy sight to last as long as possible.

"Gram! Grandad!" Scott and Walker called as they ran up to their grandparents.

Turning, Roberta and Al hugged the boys and looked over their heads at their father who had stopped several yards away. They nodded at him, although there was no accompanying smile of welcome.

"Did you see them lift off?" asked Scott, his eyes shining with excitement.

"Wasn't that awesome?" exclaimed Walker, with no less sense of wonderment.

"It was awesome," agreed Roberta.

Pulling on her arm, Walker said, "Come and say hi to Dad."

Roberta and Al exchanged a glance and let the boys lead them over to their father. Al was the first to speak.

"Hello, Ted," he said, putting out his hand. Ted hesitated a fraction of a second, and then took the offered hand, greeting his in-laws. He kept his eyes lowered.

"See that big yellow and red balloon? They let us climb in the basket before they took off!" said Walker. "It was way cool."

"You can still see it, over there, see?" Scott pointed.

The adults nodded and stood silently a moment.

"Well, we'll see you boys later," said Roberta. "Have a fun day."

As Roberta and Al turned, and the boys started off toward the hot chocolate stand, Ted cleared his throat. "I'm...I'm sorry. I'm so sorry."

They stopped and looked back at him. He added, "I want to make it right again. I'm trying to make it right."

The silence hung between them like a gauze curtain. Finally, Roberta's gaze softened. "We hope you can, Ted." She and Al walked away. Al caught her hand in his as they walked on, giving it a squeeze.

Kay, Ben and Jeremy shared the lunch from Subway while they sat on Ben's condo deck. Their conversation skirted around the main subject on all their minds as they commented on the balloons, the size of the crowd, and the beautiful weather. Actually, it was a conversation between Kay and Ben. Jeremy sat with his head lowered, his body slumped in his usual posture of defeat.

Finally, Kay approached what was in their thoughts. "Jeremy, who were those guys you were talking to at the festival. I didn't like their looks."

"Just some guys I met in Taos. I can't help how they look."

"What did they want with you? Were they threatening you in some way?" asked Ben. "That's what it looked like."

Jeremy squirmed in his seat. "What do you care? I'm not your business. You don't even really know me."

Ben nodded. "That's true. But Mrs. Tucker dared to take you in instead of turning you in to the police, though that was a very foolish, perhaps even dangerous, thing for her to do. And now I have taken you in. We have a stake in you. We care about you now."

Kay added, "Remember, Jeremy, I said I'd give you this past week and that after the balloon festival we'd have to make some decisions. Well, it's that time. I appreciate that Rev. James is here to help with those decisions. Please be honest with us and let us help you make the best plan for your future."

Jeremy sat with his head bowed. Speaking softly, he said, "You both been so good to me. I ain't never had nobody treat me like that before. I don't know why you done it. I don't understand it at all." He shook his head. "I can't hardly believe you both is real, you know? But, I don't know what to do next, where to go. I ain't got no future anywhere."

Over the boy's lowered head, Kay and Ben's glances met and shared the concern over this stranger who had ended up in their care. And in their hearts.

"I understand how you might feel that way now, Jeremy," began Ben, "but because we are older, it's easier for us to see what might be ahead for you. It's true you've messed up and you're in a bad place. If you'll be honest and forthright with us, we can help you mend what has happened in the past, and help you work toward a better future."

Jeremy finally looked up, and Kay could see that his eyes shone with unshed tears. "How?" he asked, his voice trembling with emotion. "Why?"

"I'll answer both those questions," said Ben. "First, the 'why'. Mrs. Tucker and I both believe in a God that wants us to care for each other in this world, and especially, to care for someone who is struggling, as you are. We're aware of how much he has blessed us in our lives. We have wonderful families, good health, a comfortable existence, and we live in this beautiful place. We both feel that he has led you here to give us the opportunity to help you."

Jeremy sat shaking his head in disbelief.

"Now for the 'how'," continued Ben. "We need to go back and start with when you ran away from home. That was about six months ago, right?"

Jeremy nodded.

"We'll need to be in touch with your mother and let her know where you are. How old are you, Jeremy?"

"I'm almost eighteen," he muttered, looking away.

Kay raised a questioning eyebrow as she and Ben exchanged a knowing look. "Remember I said you had to be honest with us. How old are you?" asked Kay.

"I'm sixteen," he growled, reluctantly.

"Thank you." Ben smiled at him. "So, we'll contact your mother and let her know you're safe here with me and that you will be staying with me for an indefinite time. Next, we'll get in touch with the juvenile authorities in Santa Fe, and ..."

Jeremy jumped up, slamming his fist on the table. "No way! They'll make me go back to juvie hall. Ain't no way! I'll run away again."

Ben put his hand gently on Jeremy's arm, "Sit down, son, and hear me out."

Jeremy grumbled, "I ain't your son," but he sat back down, scowling.

"It's a gamble, but with all the problems of overcrowding I think I can work out a deal. I've done this before in Texas. If I can arrange to be your guardian and we get you into some kind of community service hours here, I think it will work."

Jeremy sat silently, but the scowl left his face.

"You'll have to understand that I have strict rules you'd have to obey. There can be no drinking or drugs. Zero, and I mean that." Ben looked at Jeremy with a stern expression. "I expect you always to be honest with me. I'll give you curfew and you have to be home by that time. Do you understand?"

"Yeah, I get it."

Ben's expression was full of compassion, but Jeremy still did not look up. 'We'll see about some kind of job besides doing the community service hours. That will be your money that we'll put aside for the future."

Now Jeremy's head shot up and he glared at Ben. "Ya mean I gotta work, but I don't get to keep any of the money?"

"I'll give you part of it so you'll have some spending money, but we'll be putting a portion aside as savings for the future. Believe me, you'll need it someday for an apartment, living expenses, that kind of thing."

Kay looked from one to the other, so thankful that Ben had stepped in to help this broken boy. *What was I thinking? I could never do for him what Ben is doing. Thank you, Lord, for taking this out of my hands!*

"Tell me about when you ran away from Santa Fe? When was that and how did you get to Taos?" Ben asked, his voice softening.

Jeremy let out a deep breath, as if he was resolved to do what Ben required. "I guess that was about late in February. It was pretty cold. I hitched a ride, not headed anywhere special, just away. The guy was going to Taos, so that's where I ended up. I found lots of places to kind of camp out, you know? I went to the men's shelter once, but I was scared they'd turn me in so I never went back. I found this group of guys I could hang with, those guys you saw talking to me today." Once Jeremy started sharing, the words spilled out, faster and faster.

"They were doin' lots of sh...stuff, drugs and all. I tried some," he glanced up at Ben, then Kay to see their reaction. Seeing none, he continued. "But, I was too scared to keep on. I mean, I needed to keep it together to survive. They was also doing stuff like shoplifting, and sometimes they bragged about mugging some drunk behind the bars. I knew I was in enough trouble already without getting caught for even more. So, that's when I decided to split and come up here."

"I'm proud of you for having the courage to keep from getting more involved with those thugs. What did they want with you today?" Ben asked.

Jeremy looked away. "Uh, they was wantin' to know who might be a good mark up here with all these rich people."

"What did you tell them?"

"Nothin'! Honest." His glance met Ben's. "I didn't say nothin'. That's why they was getting mad at me, then you came along."

Kay asked, "How did you get up here?"

"I hitched a ride. Some homeless guy told me that by hanging around McDonald's in Taos you could sometimes get a free meal. I was doin' that and I heard this guy ask how far was it to Angel Fire so, I asked him for a ride. I told him I'd hitched to see my gramma in the hospital, but I needed to get back to Angel Fire, and he said

OK. He led me out to his truck. It was kinda neat, a lifted Ford F150, red with silver trim. Really sweet. He didn't ask no questions or nothin'. On the way up I asked him if he had family in Angel Fire. He said no, that he was going to hike for a few days then go to Eagle Nest and fish for a few days. I thought that was kinda weird, though, 'cause he didn't have no gear of any kind in that truck, not even a duffle bag or nothin' for clothes."

"That does seem strange. So, when did you actually get up here, Jeremy?" Ben asked.

Jeremy shrugged. "I dunno. It was probably around the middle of April. It was still cold and there was lots of rain. I hung out at that lake for a while, getting shelter where I could."

Kay looked up sharply. "You mean Eagle Nest Lake?"

"Naw. I didn't go that far. You know that lake down there," he gestured. "The one near those stables."

"That's Monte Verde Lake. Did you know that's where they found the dead woman?"

Jeremy squirmed in his seat again, looking very uncomfortable. "Uh, I heard somethin' about it."

"Did you ever see anything strange or suspicious?" Kay leaned forward.

Jeremy rubbed his arms. "Naw, I never saw nothin'"

Ben looked at Kay with a question in his eyes. She shook her head. Time enough to deal with explanations later.

"So, Jeremy, what do you think? Are you willing to work with us to get yourself on track?" Ben asked. "You would have to agree with all my rules."

"And if I don't?"

"Then it's time for you to leave, young man. You'd be on your own again. There's the door. You're free to go."

CHAPTER NINE

As Roberta began her drive to get Kay she thought, as she often did, that the valley and surrounding mountains decorated her world in so many wonderful ways. The rainfall of the spring and early summer had dressed the valley in a lush green, highlighted by the many wildflowers. The sky might be so blue and pure that it touched her soul in some deep way, or it might be foreboding danger, roiling with clouds silver, gray and black and crackling with lightning. The sky at night could be inky black, sparkling with a million stars, or tease the night watcher with a fleeting moon behind a veil of clouds. In fall, the aspens spilled their gold down the mountainsides, and winter would cast a soft, silent spell of white over her world. Whatever the season or time of day, Roberta marveled at the majesty of her surroundings.

This morning was no exception. There had been rain during the night Monday, and as Roberta headed down the mountain she saw the clouds hanging low through the valley. The tops of the mountains stood clear against the blue-gray sky, looking as if they were rising out of a mist. *Reminds me of Brigadoon,* she thought, remembering the play she had seen years ago about the place that only occasionally appeared mysteriously out of the mist.

Driving to breakfast after picking up Kay, Roberta said, "Can you tell me what's going on with that boy we met, Jeremy? I caught some strange undercurrents when Ben introduced him at the balloon festival."

Kay grimaced. "I knew I'd have to tell you eventually. OK, here's what happened. A few weeks ago, when I got home from breakfast, I found Jeremy in my house. He'd snuck in to get some food, thinking no one would be home. He's a runaway. He left a very bad home situation in Albuquerque six months ago. First, he was in Santa Fe, then Taos, and then he came up here. I let him stay in my garage for a while."

"What?" Roberta looked at her friend, surprise in her expression. "So, that's why you were locking your house all of a sudden."

Kay glanced at Roberta. "Yes, that was why." Continuing with the story she said, "One day Ben had stopped by and he saw Jeremy cleaning my deck and asked about him. Since Ben was a minister, I felt like I could tell him the truth. After that, he talked to Jeremy, and he kind of took matters into his own hands. He didn't think it was a good idea for Jeremy to be staying with me so he moved him over to his condo. He has an extra bedroom. He's good with Jeremy, knows how to be firm, set rules and all that. I couldn't have done that."

"Wow. You should never have let that boy stay at your place! What were you thinking? Amber would have had a fit if she'd found out."

"I know. I know all that, but he seemed like such a vulnerable kid. I couldn't turn him over to the police, Bertie. I couldn't. Ben is working with him to help him get straightened out. I believe he can do it. Evidently, Ben has mentored boys like this in the past. He's really good with him."

Roberta shook her head, and they drove in silence the rest of the way to the café. She was stunned that Kay had done such a foolish thing as keeping a runaway, but even more, she was a little hurt that Kay had not confided in her about the situation. *Thank goodness Ben had stepped in and was supervising the boy now!* she thought. *I wonder what this means about their relationship.*

They were the first to arrive, so they pulled the tables together, got their coffee, and were sitting down when the others arrived. The usual commotion with several conversations going on at once filled the café until their orders were taken.

Roberta thought about whose news might be the most important and she turned to Wanda. "Is there something you need to share with us?" she asked.

Wanda looked around and bit her bottom lip. Her tee shirt's joyful advice, "Never play cards in the Serengeti. There are too many cheetahs," belied her worried expression.

"I hope it's not a problem, but before I left home, I had my annual mammogram. Something showed up, so they called me back in for a sonogram. I was hopeful that would be clear, but I got a call from my doctor on Friday. There is definitely a suspicious lump. We're leaving in the morning to go back home so I can have a biopsy done."

"Oh, Wanda, I hate to hear that," said Kay, putting her hand over Wanda's.

"It sounds like you're in good hands, though," said Annabelle. "If they have found something, it's very early, which is good. There's an old Irish saying my dad used to say. 'There's no need to fear the wind if your haystacks are tied down.' "

"What in the world does that mean?" asked Myra.

"It means do what you can to be prepared for difficulties. Wanda has done that by getting the mammogram and doing the follow up the doctors said to do. She's done what needed to be done, so, logically, now the problem will be taken care of in the best possible way."

The friends nodded. There wasn't one of them that couldn't imagine what Wanda was feeling; the underlying dread; the hope that they were not joining that long parade of women who have to face breast cancer with all its ugly implications.

"I wanted you all to know. I covet your prayers, and I'll keep you posted. Hopefully, I'll be back before you know it."

There was a moment of silence around the group, but Wanda felt the circle of caring and concern surround her, and she felt that comfort that can come only from a sisterhood such as the one the JULIETs had developed.

She smiled for the first time that day. "Let's not dwell on that. We've got a mystery to solve, don't we? What's the latest, Snoop Sisters?"

Myra, Tessa and Olivia all began talking at once, then stopped, laughing at themselves. The laughter was what they needed to break the pall that had settled over the group with Wanda's news. The server brought their orders, so they waited until she had left their table to begin their conversation again.

"Well," began Myra, "I talked to Wilda over at the RV Park. She said that the victim, Bev Tensley, was very hard to get to know. They hiked together several times, but Wilda didn't learn much about her and felt like they would never become friends. Bev didn't have any children, and she had been divorced for several years. She never seemed to have any friends come to visit her cabin at Bobcat Meadows."

Tessa pulled out her cell phone. "Olivia and I spent one afternoon tracking Bev down on social media. There were some interesting things on Facebook." She tapped a few places on her phone and started scrolling down. "Here was one of the most interesting. She had posted a picture of a little adobe house about a year ago, and here's the comment she put with it. 'My ex's new house with his new wife. I know where it is, and will be watching for the little expected bundle of joy.' That sounds like a threat to me. What do you think?"

"That could simply be something she said in a moment of anguish or if she'd had too much to drink," said Roberta.

Myra nodded. "I did ask Wilda if Bev was a drinker. She said she'd never seen Bev drunk, but she knew she drank kombucha because Bev had offered her some one time."

"What is kombucha?" asked Annabelle.

"It's an herbal tea kind of thing. It's made by fermenting tea so it can have adverse reactions, but it's not intoxicating. Wilda told you that Bev liked to find natural foods and use them, didn't she?" said Olivia, remembering a previous conversation.

"Yes," said Myra. "She also said that Bev was trying to lose weight using some natural things. Wilda wasn't sure if it was something that is native around here or not."

"Was she a very overweight person?" asked Roberta.

"I don't think she was overweight at all," said Myra. "Maybe she wanted to get really slim and win her ex back."

"Judging from her Facebook entries, she did want him back. Olivia and I skimmed back several years. It sounded like she didn't want the divorce."

"I actually researched that because it got me wondering," said Tessa. "You know, you can find anything on the Internet. Here's the most interesting thing of all. The husband is the one who filed for divorce and he even had a restraining order against her."

"A restraining order? That's amazing. Do you think he was being stalked by her?" said Wanda.

"That sounds very possible," commented Annabelle. "It also might be that during the marriage he was abused by her."

Wanda looked surprised. "That's a switch."

"It is," agreed Roberta, "although I've heard of battered husbands. We always think it's the wife who is the victim."

"I'm sure the police are looking into the possibility that the victim was the abuser since there was a restraining order," said Annabelle. "What we need to be thinking about are the obscure little details that the investigation might not pick up on. After all, we know they're understaffed, and they have to send any evidence away because they're not equipped to handle it here. So, what are the minute details that we might think about?"

Myra consulted her pad. "The odd thing that the police may not even know is her interest in native plants. Perhaps it wasn't murder, but an accidental poisoning."

The group nodded as Myra looked around at them.

"But wouldn't the toxicology report have indicated that?" asked Wanda.

"Not necessarily," said Myra. "I've also been researching that on the Internet. They only look for the obvious things. I think we should pursue this. Do you know any more about kombucha, Tessa?"

"A little. It's basically a home-brewed, strong tea, but now it can be purchased in health food stores or online. It's basically harmless, but because it's usually homemade it could become too acidic or have some bacteria develop in it. If that happens, it could cause health problems, but I doubt if it would cause death. A more likely problem would have been eating the wrong mushrooms or berries, but it sounds like Bev would have known the difference."

"I wonder what she was taking to try to lose weight. Do you think we could find that out from Wilda?" said Annabelle.

"Sure. I think it's time we went and checked the cabin out. I'm sure Wilda will let us in."

"Is there still police tape around it?" asked Kay.

Myra shrugged. "But even if there is, what harm could it do if we only go in and look around. We won't touch anything or take anything out of the cabin."

"Myra, it's a crime scene! The police tape means no one can enter." Kay's expression showed her disapproval.

"Oh, I know," said Myra. "I'll get Wilda to tell us when the police tape is gone. She's pressuring them to remove it since it's hurting her business. I think they'll take it down soon, if they haven't already. After all, they've probably examined the cabin thoroughly by now. Even so, when we **can** go in, I think we should look around that cabin with fresh eyes, and something may occur to us."

Nods all around. Myra went on. "I did call the State Trooper office and was told Andy Barta is in charge of the investigation. I talked to him yesterday and told him about how we had solved the mountain bike theft. I suggested that maybe because of the locations of the cabin where the boys were found and the cabin where Bev lived there might be some connection."

"What did he say?" asked Roberta.

"Well, he thanked me for the suggestion, but I felt like he didn't take me seriously. In fact, I might say he even acted like I was an interfering busybody."

"All the more reason we should solve this," said Wanda with a rueful smile.

The friends smiled at each other, and a determined glint was in the eyes of each and every one of them.

Three days later Wanda entered the six-story hospital back in her home town. Her husband quickly joined her after parking the car. At the information desk, the woman in the pink smock instructed her to go to the waiting room down the hall and wait there to be called by one of the admitting clerks.

Walking down the hall, Wanda felt a chill. She wasn't sure if it was the sterile look of the place, the antiseptic smell, or the mere fact that she had to be there for the procedure. Wanda and Robert sat silently together on the gray chairs. The waiting room was crowded at this early hour, but conversation was muted and infrequent. Wanda pulled out her cell phone and checked for emails, knowing it wasn't likely that anyone would be emailing her so early. Still, she feigned interest in ads for a Dell computer, a vacation trip to Greece, and a sale at Woman Within's website. She tried to keep her breathing regular and to keep her hands from shaking. After all, this was only a biopsy. The results could be benign. There was no point worrying unnecessarily, right? At least, that's what she kept telling herself.

Wanda glanced at her husband, seemingly engrossed in a year-old golf magazine. She knew he was concerned, but he did not want to talk about it at all. *I wish Bertie were here!* She tried to think about the mystery they were working on. That would surely take her mind off today's procedure.

"Mrs. Smith. Wanda Smith," called a clerk. Wanda rose, smiled at Robert, and followed the woman to a tiny cubbyhole office. After a number of questions and many signatures, she returned to join her husband.

"We're supposed to go to Waiting Room A on the third floor," she told him. He stood, dumped the magazine on the nearest table and followed her to the elevators.

The silence in the elevators echoed around them. "Did they say how long you have to wait there?" he asked.

She shook her head and clutched the forms she'd been given a little tighter.

The elevator door opened and they made their way down the hall to Waiting Room A, which looked exactly like the previous one, except the chairs were dark green. Robert immediately lost himself in another magazine.

Wanda looked around the room and smiled at the woman sitting next to her, admiring the rich tone of the woman's *café au lait*-hued skin.

"This is not fun, is it?" said the woman in a soft voice.

"Not at all," agreed Wanda.

"This is the second time I've been through this," the woman said. "It's really not a difficult procedure. The worry is the worst part."

"For sure," Wanda said. "I'm trying not to imagine the worst, but that's hard."

Just then, the woman was called to the back so Wanda tried to settle herself. Her thoughts turned to Angel Fire, wishing she were there, that all this was behind her, that she was picking out one of her tee shirts to wear to Tuesday breakfast. Would they really be able to come up with ideas about the mystery? Was it an accident, or suicide, or could there actually have been a murder? She tried to imagine Bev Tensley, what she had done on that fateful day that ended so tragically for her.

Mindy walked out of her room carrying her cell phone. She joined her parents in the living room, gestured with the phone and said, "That was Ted. He asked if he could come up again this weekend to see the boys." She sat in the chair facing them and looked from one parent to the other.

After a moment's silence, Al said, "Wasn't it supposed to be every other weekend?"

"That was what we originally said, yes. But, the boys had such a great weekend with him. This weekend is Habla Tamale, and that should be a lot of fun for them. He's doing everything he can to make things right again, going to the counselor, turning his paycheck and all the finances over to me, everything."

"Are you asking us what we think about him coming up?" Roberta asked.

"I guess so."

Roberta and Al exchanged a glance and paused. Finally, Roberta said, "I think that's entirely up to you, Mindy. We'll support you in whatever you decide to do."

Mindy's lip trembled and tears came to her eyes. "Thank you, Mom. Dad. Thanks for being there for me and for providing this haven for us this summer. I want things to be the way they used to be, but I know that can't happen. I want us to be a family again. That's the only outcome that is acceptable to me. As long as Ted seems to be working toward that goal too, well, I want to be as supportive as possible." She wiped away her tears and flicked them from her fingers.

"Then I think you've already decided, darling." Roberta smiled at her daughter.

Mindy nodded, stood, and headed back to her room.

CHAPTER TEN

Roberta paused at the curve on her way to pick up Kay and took a moment to savor the view. The purple penstemon filled the meadows of the valley. This spring and early summer's rain had brought a profusion of wildflowers, and it seemed that the whole community was enjoying them. Roberta had heard people commenting on the abundance of this spiky, purple wildflower when she was at Lowe's, the post office, or church. A murder of crows lifted as one from a nearby ponderosa pine, and Roberta watched their flight curve and descend out of sight. *I wonder why it's called a 'murder'*, she mused. *I'll have to ask Annabelle or Tessa when we get to breakfast.*

Her thoughts turned to the past weekend and how much Ted's visit had meant to the boys, and Mindy, too, she had to admit. It was obvious that both Ted and Mindy were trying to rebuild their family, and Roberta prayed they would be successful. She felt so conflicted about Ted. The memories of happy family times stayed in the back of her mind, but they were clouded by the grief he had recently caused Mindy and the boys. The sense of betrayal kept overpowering the positive thoughts. In the last few weeks she had read a lot about gambling as an addiction and she understood it would be an uphill battle for Ted. She and Al had talked many nights as they nestled together in their bed, and they had agreed that they would help the young couple in any way they could.

Roberta smiled at the peaceful scene before her, her optimistic nature rising to the surface as she continued on her way to Kay's.

They were the last to arrive at the café, and someone had already set out their coffee for them. Myra almost pulled them to their seats as soon as they had placed their orders at the counter. "I've been waiting for you to get here," she began breathlessly. "I have some big news, but I wanted to tell you all at the same time."

"What is it?" asked Roberta.

"Wilda called me last night. You'll never believe this! Bev Tensley's sister and brother-in-law are coming here today to try to get some answers about Bev's death. And guess what! They're going to be staying in my basement apartment. Do you realize what that means?" She looked around the group. "We can learn all about Bev, plus hear everything Officer Barta tells them about the case. With all that extra information, we can solve this in no time!"

"Wow," said Olivia. "That's great. Are you sure they'll be staying with you? I would think they might want to stay at Bobcat Meadows."

Myra shook her head. "No way. They said it would be too creepy for them to stay there."

Conversation ended for a few moments as the server brought their food.

Tessa picked up the conversation after the server left. "This could be really helpful, not only getting some insights into Bev, but learning what the State Police know. I'm sure that's the only way we'd get any of their information."

"And in the meantime we can pursue all our ideas, too," added Olivia.

"Absolutely," said Annabelle. "I had an interesting conversation at the post office yesterday I wanted to tell you about."

"Well, the post office is the best place to get information," said Roberta with a chuckle. "It's one place where we all go so you always meet someone you know."

"This was someone I simply got into a conversation with, but I learned so much. His name is Sam Fernandez, and he's been delivering the mail here from Springer since 1974, even before we had a post office and the locals picked up their mail at the old country club."

"I didn't know they did that," said Kay. "That was even before my time here."

"Yes, before most of us. I was thinking that he probably would notice anything strange or different so I asked him what he'd heard about the murder. He really didn't have any information we didn't already know. He remembered about an earlier murder that had happened here. I had forgotten about that. It was years ago. Anyway, he has taken up photography as a hobby and in the three hours he has to fill here in Angel Fire while he's waiting for the return mail for Springer, he goes around taking pictures."

"Interesting hobby," said Olivia.

"That made me think that he might have inadvertently photographed something and there could be a clue in one of his photos." Annabelle looked around at the group. "Here's the interesting part. Many of the pictures are enlarged and are for sale at Lowe's and there's a nice large one on the wall at the Bakery. Maybe we should get out our magnifying glasses and go look at them carefully. He did give me a handful of snapshots to look at. I have to return them to him tomorrow. I think he gave them to me in the hope that I want to buy one and have it enlarged. I hate to disappoint him, so if any of you want one, please let me know." Annabelle passed the packet of pictures to Kay. "Take one each and study them carefully, then pass them around again."

Silence fell over the group as the friends considered each of the photographs.

"This one of the lake is interesting, not because it reveals any clues, but because it reminds me of how much water we had this spring." Kay tapped the photo. "This shows how all the canoes and paddleboats that were up on the shore last winter were under water this spring."

"I remember that," said Roberta. She paused, drumming her fingers as she thought. "Let's see. They said she apparently died about April 17th, right? I remember that the lake flooded soon after that because it was on our granddaughter, Elizabeth's, birthday. We called to wish her happy birthday and I was telling her all about the lake being so flooded and the canoes being out in the lake since we had gone canoeing when she was here." She passed the picture around again.

The pictures made their way around the table as each of the women studied them carefully. "I don't see anything that gives us any clues," said Tessa.

"Wait! Look at this," exclaimed Olivia. "This picture of that old cabin on the way to our church. Look really closely at the window. Doesn't it look like a face there?"

Annabelle studied the photo. "It could be, but it's hard to tell." She turned the snapshot over and read the date, "April 17th, 2015. Oh my gosh! That's the day Bev died. Could a murderer have been hiding out in that cabin? Maybe it was some homeless drifter passing through."

Kay's stomach tensed into a knot. *Where was Jeremy finding shelter in those days when he first arrived in Angel Fire? It was about that time.*

"Let's go over to Lowe's and see if this is one of the pictures that has been enlarged, Maybe we could see the detail better," suggested Roberta.

The friends finished their remaining sips of coffee and tea, gathered their purses and headed next door to Lowe's. The picture of the cabin was not one included in the display, but they carefully perused each the pictures, hoping to see something.

Walking back to their cars, Myra said, "I'll call Officer Barta before Bev's sister and brother-in-law arrive and suggest he checks out that cabin and this picture. Maybe I should take the picture to him as evidence."

Annabelle frowned slightly. "I don't know. It's not mine to give you. I have Sam's contact information. Why don't I give you that and if Officer Barta thinks it's worth pursuing, he can contact Sam himself."

"I guess that's probably the best thing to do. I need to get home anyway to get ready for my company." Myra paused. "I hate to wait until next Tuesday to report on all I'll learn from Bev's sister. Why don't you all come for coffee Thursday morning?"

Several nodded, but Kay said, "Thursday is Bible Study at the United Church of Angel Fire. Richard Safford does such a great job that I hate to miss it. Could we meet on Friday instead?"

"Friday is good," said Myra. "In fact, that might be better because I'll probably learn more by then." They all agreed to that plan, and each left feeling a little more enthusiastic about being "Snoop Sisters."

Wanda and Robert had arrived early for the appointment with her internist. They had debated whether or not Robert needed to be with her to get the results of the biopsy. She wanted to believe that everything would be fine, that the tumor was benign. If that was true then there was no need for Robert to be with her. But what if it was malignant? Then decisions would need to be made, arrangements settled on. If that were the case, she definitely needed Robert by her side.

There was no point even looking at a magazine. She wondered how Robert could be so engrossed in a Family Circle magazine, but he was only flipping through the pages.

"Wanda Smith," the nurse announced from the doorway. Wanda and Robert jumped up and followed her down the hall. It felt comforting to feel Robert's hand on the small of her back as he walked with her. The doctor was not in his office, but they only waited a moment until he entered.

He sat behind his cluttered mahogany desk and opened the file that was on top of several others. It seemed like minutes passed while he scanned the information there, but finally, he looked up smiling. "Wanda, the biopsy came back negative. We will watch the cyst, of course, but the good news is that it is not a malignancy."

Wanda and Robert seemed to let out their breath together, as if they had been holding it the whole time. They looked at each other, matching smiles. The doctor made some more remarks about follow-up appointments, but Wanda hardly heard him. As they left the doctor's office Wanda's first thought was, *I can't wait to email the JULIETs*. She knew they would be rejoicing with her.

In the elevator, Robert kissed her cheek. "Let's get back to Angel Fire," he said.

"Amen!" was all Wanda needed to reply.

As soon as Kay arrived home, she punched in Ben's cell phone number. When it went to his voice mail she said, "Please call me when you have a minute. I need to talk to you." She tried not to sound frantic, but she had had a very bad feeling ever since she had seen the picture of a face in the window of the cabin. Jeremy had been vague about where he stayed before she let him camp out in her garage but, Jeremy was vague about everything. She had never considered he might be a murderer, but she really didn't know him at all. And, maybe it wasn't a murder at all, but an accident of some kind. Even if an accident had caused Bev's death and Jeremy was somehow involved he wouldn't, of course, have been in a position to report it.

Kay knew that Ben and Jeremy were hiking with the Trekkers today – part of Ben's program to get Jeremy more physically fit – but she couldn't remember which trail they were going on so she had no idea of how long they would be.

Moments later her phone chimed, alerting her to a message. *That was fast,* she thought. She quickly saw the message was a group email from Wanda with the wonderful news of her test results. Kay offered a quick prayer of gratitude and rejoiced in the relief those results brought with them.

As soon as Myra got home she made the call to the State Trooper office, asking to speak to Officer Barta.

"Officer Barta speaking," a voice barked into the phone.

"Officer Barta, this is Myra Stanhope. My friends and I are the ones that solved the puzzle of the missing mountain bikers, and I've talked to you earlier with a suggestion about the latest mysterious death in Angel Fire."

"Yes, I remember you well."

Myra wasn't sure about his tone of voice, but she continued. "Well, I have another possible clue for you."

There was no comment from Officer Barta so Myra rushed on. "My friends and I were looking at some pictures by Sam Fernandez." Thinking that Officer Barta might not know Mr. Fernandez, Myra filled him in on the background, giving a detailed history. She paused, but there was still no comment.

"Are you still there, Officer Barta?"

With the sound of rustling papers in the background, he said, "Yes, Mrs. Stanhope. I'm still here."

"So," said Myra, "we were looking at a picture of that abandoned cabin that's in a field off West Ridge Road. Do you know the one I mean? It's on the way to our church, the United Church of Angel Fire, you know, the church with the red roof? Of course, there's the Catholic Church there now, too. They just built their church. The Catholics worked so hard raising money for the last eight years. They did things like bake sales and such. One of their most successful things was a '50s dance they have every year. Even people who might not dance any more go to it because the music is so good."

"Mrs. Stanhope," cut in Officer Barta. "Please get to the point."

"I was trying to. Well, we were looking at a picture of that cabin taken on April 17th and we think there might be a face in the window. It could have been some vagrant going through town, staying at the cabin. He might have been involved with Bev Tensley's death."

Before responding, Officer Barta gave a deep sigh. "Thank you for the information. We will check out the cabin. Goodbye, Mrs. Stanhope."

"Wait! Don't you want the contact information for Sam Fernandez? I have it right here. You should check out all his pictures. You might see a clue in one of them."

Another sigh. "All right. What is that information?"

After giving Sam's email and phone number, Myra hung up the phone, frowning. "I don't think that young man appreciates the information and help we're giving him," she muttered to herself. She shrugged and went to the basement to make the bed up fresh for her expected company.

Olivia had picked up Tessa that morning, and they sat talking in the car in Tessa's driveway before saying goodbye.

"What do you really think about our working on this mystery?" asked Tessa.

Olivia gave a slight smile. "Well, it sounds like a crazy idea, but I do think it's fun. I love mysteries and puzzles, and all that. Do you remember that my sister-in-law and I did that murder mystery weekend at the St. James Hotel a few years ago? It was so much fun, and she and I analyzed everything and figured out the murderer and why it happened."

"Oh, yeah. I remember. It took the whole weekend, didn't it?"

"Uh huh. They tell you the character you're supposed to be and you come with your costume. You stay in character all weekend. They set up the scenes, and some people have specific things to do while others only act according to their character. Each scene has some clues in it so the plot unfolds throughout the weekend. It's pretty clever."

"Who were you supposed to be?" asked Tessa.

"I was Dirty Dora, a homeless person in Cimarron. I was supposed to be loud and obnoxious, and that was really fun." Olivia chuckled, remembering.

"But, this might have been a real murder. Every now and then, I have twinges of concern. I mean, there could be a murderer out there somewhere who doesn't want to get caught. What if he – or she – finds out we're snooping around. Do you think we might be in any danger?"

Olivia paused a moment before answering. "No, I don't think so. After all, the murderer doesn't know what we're doing, and we pass our clues on to the police to do the actual work of investigating. I think we're perfectly safe. It's a good way to use our brains. Who knows, we might even come up with something."

Both phones dinged, indicating an email. Seeing the message from Wanda their conversation about the murder was left behind.

"What a relief!" exclaimed Tessa. "I know they must have been so worried."

"For sure. Breast cancer seems to be so common. I wish they could find a cure. Of course, it's such a complicated issue, not just one disease and all that. I'm glad more and more attention is going to the research." Olivia put her phone away. "I know you work on that race we have to raise money and awareness. I'll never run in it, but I always walk."

"I know, and the important thing is to be part of it."

The two sat in silence for a moment. Tessa looked at her friend. "Did I tell you that Jim and I are thinking of taking in a foster child?"

"No. You are? What a neat thing to do. You and Jim will be wonderful as foster parents," Olivia said.

"I hope so, if we decide to go ahead with it. We've started the process, but we're not one hundred per cent sure we'll do it. There's a lot to consider, and we don't want to take a child until we're positive we can do it."

"I'm sure you'll make the right decision," said Olivia.

Tessa opened the car door. "Thanks, and thanks for the ride. See you later," she said as she slipped out. Walking to her front door, she thought, *I have to admit, I never thought that becoming a foster parent would be such a difficult decision.*

CHAPTER ELEVEN

Wanda and Robert drove through the morning without much conversation. Leaving I-25 and cutting through Las Vegas, Robert asked, "Where do you want to stop for lunch?"

Wanda shrugged. "I don't care. Do you want to wait and get lunch at Mora? We could eat at Hatcha's."

"Sounds good."

She glanced at her husband. "One good thing about this trip was that we got in a quick visit with Mason."

"I always love seeing Mason," Robert replied, "but the best thing about this trip was the good report from the doctor."

"Well, of course. That was such a relief."

"I've got to admit it, hon, I was scared to death. I don't know what I would do if anything like that happened to you."

The heavy weight that had sat on them, making it hard to breathe normally for weeks, was lifted. It was as if now that they put voice to it, used words to acknowledge it, they could finally push it away. Tears burned in Wanda's eyes, but she blinked them back. Her voice was barely above a whisper. "I was scared, too."

Robert kept his eyes on the road ahead. His hands gripped the steering wheel more tightly. "I've always felt like we were invincible or something, you know? The worst thing that had ever happened in our whole lives was that Mason was autistic, and that seemed manageable somehow. There were things we could all do to make it better. But, cancer. People are fighting cancer all the time. Sometimes they win but sometimes, no matter how hard they fight, they don't win. I don't want to be one of those couples, Wanda. I don't."

She patted his leg. "I don't either. For now, we don't have to worry about it. Let's simply accept that wonderful gift and go on with life. This is a wake-up call to live in the moment, isn't it?"

He finally glanced at her and smiled as their eyes met. "And I'm sure you'll find a tee shirt for that, won't you?"

As they began the first ascent into the mountains their laughter spilled out through the open car windows and was carried into the fresh air, taking with it their weeks of anguish and worry. A hawk darted through the pines, but the ground squirrel scurried to his hole in the nick of time. And life went on.

Kay finished setting out placemats and silverware on the deck table. She took a moment to watch the hummingbirds hover by the bird feeder with the sweetened water, and marveled at how tiny they were and at the frantic motion of their wings.

Back in the kitchen, she brought out the plate of sandwiches and the bowl of potato salad from the refrigerator and set them on the counter. "They probably want chips, too," she said, thinking out loud, and she went to the pantry for a bag of potato chips. She dumped the chips into a bowl and set them beside the rest of the lunch. The doorbell rang, right on time, and she hurried to answer it.

"Ben. Jeremy. Come in," she welcomed them. "We'll go sit on the deck. It's such a beautiful day."

She thought Ben looked especially handsome today with a sky blue shirt bringing out the blue of his eyes. He smiled at her. "We didn't want to come empty handed, so Jeremy picked out these cookies for you at Lowe's."

Jeremy handed her an unwrapped package of Oreos. He shuffled from one foot to another, as if not quite knowing what to do with his arms and legs.

Kay squeezed his arm and took the cookies. "Thank you, Jeremy. Are these your favorite?"

He shrugged. "I guess."

"Well, come on through the kitchen. You can help me carry the food out." She led the way and, after getting drinks for everyone, they settled themselves around the table on the deck.

Jeremy grabbed a sandwich off the serving plate and lifted it to his mouth.

Ben laid a hand on the boy's arm, stopping him before the first bite. He smiled at Jeremy and said, "Blessing first, remember?"

Jeremy slapped the sandwich back on the plate and bowed his head, and Kay noted he blushed slightly. *Is this the same boy who broke into my house?* she marveled. She, too, bowed her head as Ben said the blessing.

After some small talk about the beautiful weather, Kay sat back and asked, "Well, have you all worked out a plan for Jeremy?"

Ben nodded. "We're making some good progress, I think. I've talked to Jeremy's mother on the phone, and we've agreed that it's probably better for Jeremy to remain here with me for now."

"I told you she don't want me there," Jeremy muttered, turning slightly to look at Kay. It was all Kay could do to keep from putting her arms around the boy, holding him close, wanting to pour some love into his broken heart, but she knew Jeremy could not accept that.

Ben continued, "And I have spoken to the director at the Juvenile Detention Center in Santa Fe and to the person who would be Jeremy's case worker. When I explained all the circumstances around his running away in the first place and also what happened in Santa Fe, they were willing to work with me to develop a plan."

He paused and looked at Jeremy, who finally looked up and met his gaze. "Jeremy and I are working on some possibilities for community service. Once we've decided, we'll make a formal proposal. I don't think we'll have any trouble getting the authorities to accept it."

"What kinds of things are you thinking of for community service projects?" asked Kay.

"Ben heard about the Firewood Angels who cut wood all year to give to people who need it for heat in the winter. I'd kinda like to do that. Ben said it would be a good workout to build muscles." Jeremy almost let himself smile, and the possibility of that smile warmed Kay's heart.

"We also thought about helping with ALM, either the unloading when the truck comes up to the food bank at the Baptist Church, or with the delivery of the food each week. They could use the help of a strong young person," said Ben.

"Those sound like two very good ideas. What about school in the fall?" Kay looked from Ben to Jeremy. Jeremy's head went down again, and his shoulders sagged.

"School isn't Jeremy's strong suit, but we're looking into some possibilities. We may work something out individually so that Jeremy could eventually get a GED."

Kay nodded at Jeremy. "Jeremy, you probably can't see it from your point of view, but it's really good to be a high school graduate. It will be very important for your future, especially when you go out job hunting."

"Yeah, yeah, that's what Ben says all the time," Jeremy grumbled. "But there's plenty of jobs I could get."

"Maybe," said Kay. "But there are a lot more possibilities when you have that diploma. I was a teacher for many years. I could help you with your assignments." Jeremy seemed about to say something but stopped. He pulled some chips from the bowl and started to munch on them.

"We may take you up on that," said Ben. He smiled that smile again at Kay. She liked the way it crinkled up his eyes.

"There's another sandwich left, Jeremy. Do you want it?" Kay passed the plate to Jeremy.

"Uh, sure," he said as he reached for the last sandwich. "Thanks," he added.

Kay took a sip of her water, wondering how to bring up the subject, and finally deciding simply to ask Jeremy.

"I want to ask you about something, Jeremy. I'm not trying to cause you a problem or anything. I'm only asking to learn something that might be important. When you first came up here to Angel Fire did you, by any chance, seek shelter at that old, abandoned cabin on the way to the two churches on West Ridge Road?"

Ben looked puzzled by Kay's question, and Jeremy's expression became wary. "Huh, why'd you ask that?" he said.

"It's just that in a photograph taken of that cabin back in April, there is a face in the window. I wondered if it might have been your face."

"And what if it was? Does someone wanna get me for tresspassin'?"

"Oh, no, nothing like that. No. I only wanted to know if you were there then."

"What's this about, Kay?" asked Ben.

Kay sighed. "I think that, because of that picture, the State Trooper who is investigating about the body of that woman pulled from the lake is going to be checking out whoever might have been in the cabin at that time. If it was Jeremy, I thought he needed to be prepared to answer any questions Officer Barta might have."

Ben put his hand on Jeremy's arm, as if to keep him from bolting. "It's OK, son. Don't get upset." For once, Jeremy didn't mutter, "I'm not your son."

"It's not a bad reflection on you, Jeremy," said Kay hastily. "We already know you were here in Angel Fire then. It's only that you may have seen someone else staying there, or hanging around. That information could help with the investigation. I wanted to alert you that the investigating officer may be getting in touch with you."

Ben kept his hand on Jeremy's arm, and Kay realized what a sense of security and stability Ben had become for the boy.

"Is that cabin where you stayed, Jeremy?" asked Ben.

Jeremy nodded. "I went there first 'cause it looked like a good, dry place," he said. "But after I'd been there a couple of hours, this other dude, a drifter, came in. He'd been stayin' there for a while, I guess. I could tell other people had been there before me, so I guess it was an easy place to find, coming off the highway." He paused and looked at Ben, who nodded for him to continue.

"This other guy, he kinda scared me. He acted like he wasn't all there or somethin', you know? I seen lots a guys like that since I been on the street, like maybe they hear other voices in their heads. So, I decided to move on."

"What did you do then?" asked Kay.

"I wandered around some. Angel Fire's got tons of houses that are empty and you can get out of the rain under the decks. There was so much rain when I first come up here."

"That's very true," said Kay.

"Well, this is not a problem for you, Jeremy," assured Ben. "I will be in touch with this Officer Barta and explain everything to him."

"Will I hafta go talk to him, too?" asked Jeremy.

"Probably, but that is nothing for you to worry about. You are simply being a helpful citizen in providing information that might aid them in an investigation."

Jeremy sat with slumped shoulders, shaking his head. "You just don't know," he muttered. "They'll find somethin' to pin on me, and I'll be back in Juvie before you know it."

Kay and Ben exchanged a worried glance over Jeremy's head.

Kay wished she had never had to bring up the subject. She said, "I can understand why you feel that way, Jeremy. When you were on your own, that kind of thing could happen more easily. But now you have an advocate. Ben is someone who understands how the world works, and he is respected. When he stands up for you, and you haven't done anything wrong, you will not be punished. You're safe with him on your side."

Jeremy slammed his palms on the table and stood up. "Safe? I never been safe a day in my life!" He stormed down the steps of the deck and walked around the corner of the house out of sight.

"Should one of us go after him?" asked Kay.

"No, he'll be back in a little bit. He needs to process all this in his own way." Ben pulled open the package of Oreos and took one out, then passed the package to Kay. "Dessert?"

"You are so calm and understanding with him," Kay said. "How do you do it?"

Ben brushed the cookie crumbs from his fingers. "I've had lots of practice. My wife and I took in foster kids, some in a lot worse shape than Jeremy. These kids are so wounded. You saw them in your classroom, I'm sure. It takes a lot to make them whole again. Some never can get there, I'm afraid."

"It breaks my heart," said Kay.

"Jeremy owes you a big debt for what you did for him, Kay. That was a risk for you. I'm not sure I could have done it if I had been in your place."

The two sat silently for a moment. "What kind of bird is that?" asked Ben, pointing to a grayish bird with russet on its back at the bird feeder.

"It's a junco," said Kay. "They like those sunflower seeds."

As they turned back to the table, Jeremy's head appeared coming up the steps. He plopped down in his chair. Ben passed the Oreos to him and said, "Have a cookie."

Jeremy opened up the package and pulled out four cookies. "Thanks," he said.

Myra looked around the living room to be sure everything was in order. She walked to the couch and plumped up the throw pillows once more. *There,* she thought, *they should feel perfectly comfortable here.* She knew that making people at ease was a big part of their willingness to open up and share their stories. And Myra was an expert at getting people to share their stories with her. She smiled to herself. *Having those cherry almond scones fresh from the oven won't hurt, either.*

The sound of tires on the gravel driveway brought Myra to the front door. Before the couple had stepped from their car, Myra had the door open and a welcoming smile on her face.

A tired looking couple slowly got out of the car. Bev Tensley's sister, Martha, was of medium height and build. Her dark brown, wavy hair was cut short and brushed back from her face, and her brown eyes carried a wary expression. Although probably only in her early forties, her face was grooved with deep wrinkles. *Bet she's a smoker,* thought Myra. *Darn. I'll have to make sure she doesn't smoke inside.*

Hank, her husband was not much taller than his wife. His Hawaiian print shirt was buttoned tightly over a rather large paunch, but thin, bird-like legs showed from beneath his khaki shorts and the picture was completed by his white socks and sandals.

Myra bustled out to them, introducing herself and welcoming them. "Come in. Come in and relax for a little bit. We can get you settled in your apartment later." Myra beckoned them into the house. She noticed that Hank was breathing heavily as he passed her on the steps.

Twenty minutes later, the couple was sitting comfortably in Myra's living room, sipping coffee, eating scones, and chatting freely. At least, Martha was chatting. Her husband had managed to get a few words in, but he was content to enjoy the scones.

Myra had expressed her sympathy right away, but then the conversation had shifted to small talk, their trip to Angel Fire, the weather, their jobs back in Oklahoma.

Myra was ready to bring the conversation around to Bev Tensley. There was so much she wanted to learn about this woman whose life had ended so tragically.

After refilling the coffee cups, Myra sat back on the couch next to Martha. She turned to face her more directly. "I'd like to hear about Bev. Tell me what your sister was like."

Martha let out a big sigh and leaned toward Myra. Myra could tell that she was ready to talk.

And Myra was more than ready to listen.

CHAPTER TWELVE

Mindy walked into the house after taking the boys to the tennis courts for the tennis clinic. "Mom," she called. "Where are you?"

"In the laundry room," Roberta answered.

Mindy came in and leaned against the doorframe. "Mom, Ted texted me while I was driving home. He wants to talk to you, Dad and me when he's here next weekend. Without the boys."

Roberta paused while pulling the dry sheets from the dryer. "Talk to us. What for?"

"He didn't say. I really don't know."

Mindy moved forward to help her mother fold the sheets. "Ted and I have made a lot of progress in putting our lives back together. Maybe he wants your blessing on that."

"Surely, he knows he would have our blessing. He must know we want nothing but the happiness of you and the boys. Whatever that takes is what we want for you."

"He knows. Maybe he needs to hear it from you and Dad. I don't know, Mom. But can you make time for us to talk together this weekend?"

"Of course. Maybe when the boys go the Movies Under the Stars at the country club. Would that work?"

The two put the last fold in the sheet, the unconscious teamwork that had been an integral part of their lives as mother and daughter. "That will be fine. I'll tell your dad," said Roberta, pulling out the next sheet.

Friday morning Roberta picked Kay up on the way to Myra's. "Do you think that Myra will have a full report for us today?" asked Roberta.

Kay chuckled. "I feel sure she will. I have to admit, I'm as anxious to learn about this mysterious Bev as anyone. Myra really had us pegged when she had us start being the "Snoop Sisters.""

"I agree. This has become so interesting. Al is against our getting involved, I'm afraid. He thinks it's none of our business, plus it might be dangerous if we get snooping too closely and there's a murderer out there who doesn't want to be found."

"But that's what makes it interesting," said Kay. "By the way, I did ask Jeremy about where he stayed when he first got here, and he had been at that cabin. Another drifter was there, though, and Jeremy left. Ben is going to talk to Officer Barta and let him know those facts."

"I've seen Ben and Jeremy around town together. He seems to be handling that boy very well," said Roberta.

"Oh, he is. Honestly, Bertie, I don't know what I was thinking when I considered letting Jeremy stay with me. He needs so much more structure and discipline. Ben is wonderful with him. He told me that he and his wife had taken in lots of foster children over the years, and it's obvious that Ben is gifted in handling kids like Jeremy."

Roberta eased the car into Myra's driveway behind Olivia's Bronco. "Well, let's go learn all the latest," she said.

Myra had the coffeepot ready and another plate of scones plus lemon poppy muffins sitting on the coffee table. Olivia and Tessa were already seated on the couch, and Annabelle and Wanda soon arrived. They all jumped up to hug Wanda.

"We are all so relieved and happy for you, Wanda," said Kay, expressing what was in each of their hearts.

"Well, we certainly were relieved. I feel so lucky. A scare like that makes a person appreciate good health so much more. I had to wear this appropriate tee shirt for today." She smiled as they all read its message, "Middle age is when you finally get your head together and your body starts falling apart."

"Amen," said Roberta, who had started the day with a couple of ibuprofens.

The group settled themselves again and looked at Myra to begin.

"Are they downstairs?" whispered Wanda.

Myra shook her head as she pulled up a chair. "They've gone to Taos for the day."

"Have you learned much about Bev?" asked Tessa.

"Oh, yes." Myra picked up the notebook from the table. "I made notes of the important things after I went to bed last night. Here's what Martha told me. Bev was the younger sister, four years younger. There were no other siblings, and they have different fathers. Neither father was ever in the picture. I'm not sure they even knew who their fathers were."

"How sad," said Kay.

"It gets sadder," said Myra. "They lived several places in New Mexico and Texas when they were young, depending on where the mother's latest boyfriend took them. Then when Bev was about six, their mom got very sick and put them in the state's care."

"Was that in Texas?" asked Olivia.

"Uh huh. From then on they were in the foster care system. Some of it was OK, and some was terrible. From the time Bev was in middle school until she graduated they were in the worst one. The foster parents weren't so bad, but there was another foster child there, a boy, who was really abusive especially toward Bev. Of course, Martha was released from foster care when she was eighteen, but Bev stayed there another four years."

"Abusive in what way?" asked Annabelle.

Myra grimaced. "I'm sure physically and emotionally. Maybe even sexually. I don't know. Martha didn't want to get specific, and I didn't want to push her. She said he was a big kid, called him a 'tank', so I guess he was quite a bully."

"It's easy to see why Bev may have become an abusive person herself," said Roberta. "Were Bev and her sister close?"

"From everything she told me, I think they were very close when they were younger. After all, they had to depend on each other. They didn't really have anyone else. It seems as though when they got older, especially after they each married, they kept in touch off and on. She did say she hadn't actually seen Bev for about two years, although they often talked on the phone or emailed."

"What else did her sister say about her?" asked Annabelle.

Myra glanced at her notes. "Well, she said it was obvious they didn't have the same two parents because they didn't look anything alike. She told me that Bev was very petite, although she struggled to keep her weight down. She described Bev as very strong-willed. She said she was 'feisty', and that she wouldn't take any guff from anybody. She said that Bev would really stand up to Zack, the foster brother. In fact, she said that Bev swore that someday she'd get even with him for all the bad things he did to her. Evidently, he was a very disturbed young man."

"Didn't the foster parents ever protect Bev from that boy?" asked Kay.

"I don't think so. It sounded like the parents sort of ignored the kids."

"That's terrible!" Tessa exclaimed. "This isn't the best time, but I've been wanting to tell you all that Jim and I are thinking of becoming foster parents."

Myra beamed at her. "Good for you. You both would be wonderful foster parents."

Tessa shrugged. "I don't know. It's such a responsibility. We're looking at it from all aspects. We haven't decided for sure yet."

"You should talk to Ben," said Kay. "He and his wife were foster parents for many children, and he's acting in that capacity – unofficially – with Jeremy. He knows a lot about it."

"Thanks, Kay. We will talk to him. That would be so helpful to us."

Myra turned a page in her notebook. "Let's see. What else? Oh, the part about Bev being so interested in natural foods, berries and mushrooms and all, well, Martha said that's kind of new. She started that interest only about three years ago. She was very interested in natural supplements, you know, herbs and minerals and things instead of medicines."

"Did you learn anything about her marriage?" asked Annabelle.

"Martha liked Bev's husband. Bev and Mike Tensley had a whirlwind romance and married at a wedding chapel in Las Vegas. It wasn't long, though, before they started bickering about everything."

"Did Martha say anything about whether or not Bev was abusive to her husband? That is so hard for me to imagine." Roberta shook her head.

Myra shrugged. "I tried to come around to that very subtly and I never got a firm answer. I think from several things she said that it must have been true, though. I don't think the husband was abusive to Bev. He was the one who filed for divorce and, evidently, Bev was devastated by that. She tried to keep in touch with him but about a year and a half ago, he remarried. Martha did tell me that when Bev learned he and his new wife were expecting a baby, she went to pieces. Somehow, until that time, she had hoped they would get back together, I guess."

"It sounds like Bev had a very hard life," commented Annabelle. "It's sad. It makes me determined to do the best for her by discovering what led to her tragic death." Nods all around.

"I agree," said Kay. "Thanks, Myra, for getting us into this."

Myra was flustered for a moment, then smiled at everyone. She set the notebook on the table. "Well, where do we go from here, ladies?"

"I'm interested in the foster brother as a possible suspect. Perhaps they met up again somehow, and it went bad. Can you get his full name from Bev's sister, Myra? I can research him on the web."

Myra made a notation on her notebook. "I'll text you as soon as I find out."

"Is the police tape still around the cabin? I think it would be good for us to look through the cabin. I'm sure it will be cleaned out of Bev's things very soon," said Annabelle.

"You're right," agreed Myra. "Martha was going out the first of next week to collect everything. I'll call Wilda. Shall I arrange for us to go in the morning?"

Annabelle held up a finger. "I have an idea. Why don't you suggest to Martha that we pack up all Bev's things for her and bring them to her at your house? That way, it will relieve her of the stress of having to go to the cabin and seeing things as Bev left them."

"Very good idea," said Kay. "Then we'll have an excuse to go through every little thing."

Annabelle nodded. "Right. Plus, it does make it easier for Martha. She can go through her sister's things when she does feel up to it, not because she has to."

"So, what do you all think really happened to Bev?" asked Roberta. "Was she hit in the head and dropped in the lake, or was there some kind of accident?"

"I think either the ex-husband did it or maybe the foster brother. I think the ex was worried she might do something to his new little family," said Tessa.

"Well, I think it was accidental poisoning from some mushroom or something, and in her confusion, she fell into the lake," suggested Wanda.

"It could have been that homeless drifter's face we saw in the picture," added Olivia.

"Let's wait and gather more evidence," said Annabelle. "You know what they say on those TV shows if an investigator tries to fit the evidence to whatever he or she believes. We want to be good investigators and simply uncover the truth, whatever it is."

Ben put an arm around Jeremy's shoulder as they entered the police station. Every aspect of the boy, his expression, his body language, his gait, reflected his reluctance at being there.

"You're here to share the facts you know, Jeremy, nothing more. When you aren't breaking any laws, you have nothing to be afraid of. I'll be right by your side. Don't worry."

When the police chief ushered them into the conference room, Ben was surprised at how young Officer Barta looked. They shook hands after the introductions and settled themselves into the folding chairs on each side of the table. Jeremy kept his head lowered.

Ben spoke first. "As I explained on the phone, Jeremy is under my guardianship temporarily. His background is not relevant to this case you're investigating, but because he had some observations, we thought it was important that he share them with you."

"We are interested in anything that might pertain to this case," said Officer Barta. Looking at Jeremy with a stern expression, he continued. "I understand that you stayed a short while at that abandoned cabin on West Ridge Road."

"Yes, sir," mumbled Jeremy.

"Was that when you first came to Angel Fire?"

Jeremy nodded. "Yeah. I mean, yes, sir."

"And when was that. Do you know the date?"

Shrugging, Jeremy said, "I don't know 'xactly. I had no cause to pay attention to dates or nothin'."

Chief McCaslin asked, "Can you estimate the month and approximate time of the month?"

"Well, I know it was April. Let me think. I 'member this guy who gave me a ride from Taos asked if I had my taxes done. I didn't know what he was talkin' 'bout, and he said 'cause it had been tax day on Wednesday or somethin'."

Ben nodded. "Income taxes are due April 15th. That's good, Jeremy. So, was the 15th the day you came up?"

Jeremy closed his eyes as he thought. "Nah. It weren't the day of taxes. Probably a couple of days later. I'd guess it was a Friday."

"So, you would have come up on the 17th?" asked Officer Barta.

"I guess."

The two law enforcement officers exchanged a glance. Considering the estimated time of death was April 17th, they became a lot more interested in Jeremy.

Officer Barta clicked his pen open and tapped his notebook. "So, tell me about your moves from the time you left Taos on April 17th.

"I hitched a ride from McDonalds in Taos with some guy who was comin' up here to hike and fish, he said. He dropped me off at the blinking light. I was walkin' down that road and I saw that cabin. Since it looked like it was 'bout to rain, I decided to hole up there. It was pretty dry."

Officer Barta interrupted. "Was it empty?"

"I thought it was, but this weird dude came in. He was a drifter, I guess."

"That would have been April 17th still?" said Officer Barta, making a note.

Jeremy shrugged. "I guess. Anyways, he kinda freaked me out, so I left."

Ben turned toward Jeremy. "Why don't you tell them about the truck you rode up in and what was odd about what the driver told you."

Jeremy looked puzzled. "The truck was pretty neat, a lifted red Ford 150 with silver trim."

"Jeremy told me that the man driving said he was coming here for several days to hike and then fish at Eagle Nest, but he didn't have anything with him," Ben explained to the officers.

"Oh, yeah. He didn't have no gear or duffle bag for clothes or nothin'."

Officer Barta lifted his pen and scratched his head with it. "So, what did you do after you left the cabin?"

Jeremy related what he had told Kay and Ben, that he had huddled under decks when it was raining and at night, and he had gotten most of his food from dumpsters. As Ben had previously instructed him, Jeremy simply told about meeting up with Kay, her inviting him to stay in her garage, and finally, meeting Ben and going with him.

"I think that's all we need right now. You're free to go, but don't leave town in case we want to talk to you again, understand?" Officer Barta got to his feet.

"He won't be going anywhere, Officer. We're happy to cooperate in any way," Ben said as they stood.

After Ben and Jeremy left, Officer Barta commented, "Well, that jives with what that Mrs. Stanhope told me, that someone was at that cabin. I checked it out and no one had been there for quite a while. I doubt if there's any way we can trace the drifter. It's possible he connected with the victim someway and he drowned her in the lake, but it's a pretty long shot."

"Yeah, that's a very cold trail," said the chief.

"But that boy's not off the hook in my view. He can't really account for himself around the time of the death. I'll be keeping an eye on him." Officer Barta flipped his notebook closed and put it and the pen in his pocket.

CHAPTER THIRTEEN

Saturday's sky was deep blue with not even a puff of a cloud. Ted and the two boys got a very early start for the Taos Ski Valley to begin their hike up to Wheeler Peak. Al also left early for a tee time with his usual foursome. Mindy and a friend had gone to Eagle Nest to browse the shops there and have lunch at Kaw-lija's. Roberta had sensed Mindy's uneasiness about Ted's request to talk to the three of them, and she had to confess, she felt the same way. *What could he want to talk to us about?* she had wondered over and over. Roberta was glad to have a special activity this morning herself. *Maybe it will make the time go by faster.* She picked Kay up and they met the other JULIETs at the Visitor Center parking lot.

As they gathered to divide into two cars, Tessa reported, "I did a lot of research on the foster brother, Zack Sadowsky. You won't believe this but he lives in Taos. I found him on Facebook, and he's quite the ladies' man or, at least, he presents himself as one. Personally, I think he must be a big loser. He works as a bartender. I'll bet the picture he used is years old. I suspect from some of his comments and some of his friends that he's into porn, so I don't think he's changed much since they were together in that foster home."

"That is very important information. We need to tell that to Officer Barta. I'm sure he would never think to check out another person who happened to be in the same foster home so many years ago. We'll have to get Martha to call him. Good work, Tessa," exclaimed Myra.

"Do you think the police suppose that Bev died by an accident, falling and hitting her head?" Kay wondered.

Myra shrugged. "Who knows what they think. They've only told Martha those bare facts that we already saw in the newspaper. I think they don't believe a murder could happen up here so they're not pushing to find facts that indicate it was a murder. They expect Officer Barta to simply give up and say there are no clues so it must have been an accident. We can't let that happen for Bev's sake. Or for Martha's."

After settling themselves in two cars, they headed for the Bobcat Meadows RV Park and Cabins. "I brought several boxes and some grocery bags to pack things in," said Myra. "Martha was very happy that we are doing this. She said that she couldn't face going into that cabin."

"It works well for all of us," said Kay, "although I can't imagine that we'll find anything the police didn't."

"Maybe not, but I wouldn't be surprised for two reasons if we don't uncover some clue. One, that Officer Barta is very young. I suspect this is his first case to investigate and they gave him this one because they don't think much could happen here in Angel Fire. And, two, because we're such good detectives and we each bring a different perspective, a different way of seeing things. One of us is bound to see something interesting." Myra smiled at her analysis.

Annabelle and Olivia were sitting in the backseat of Tessa's car. Annabelle turned toward Olivia. "How are things going with your mother?"

Olivia sighed. "They're about the same, I guess, so that's good. At least we're not seeing more signs of the dementia. It's as if Mom has plateaued at this beginning stage."

"I know it's very sad for you to see it happening," said Annabelle.

"It really is. Mom was always so bright and energetic, so with it. Some days, she's still that way. It's the not knowing what to expect with each visit that kind of throws me."

"I can understand," said Annabelle. "Remember that the love between a mother and daughter is forever, no matter what the outward circumstances are."

Olivia's smile was wistful. "I'll try to remember that. Thanks."

The two cars pulled up by the cabin that had been Bev Tensley's home. Wilda Acker, the manager met them at the door and unlocked it. "Thanks for clearing out all Bev's things," she said. "I want to get this cabin back to where I can rent it out again."

"We shouldn't be too long," Myra said, handing out cartons to the JULIETs. Once inside, the group split up. The cabin consisted of a main room with a faded brown plaid sofa, matching chair, and an oak coffee table. A small TV sat perched on a metal stand along one wall. Over the TV two framed prints of aspen trees were hanging with a slight tilt. Green and white gingham curtains covered the window of one wall, and a small galley kitchen filled the space across from it. Tessa, Olivia and Annabelle went to the bedroom just off the main room. Roberta, Kay, and Wanda started on the kitchen. Myra began boxing up things from the main room. The friends worked quietly, making occasional comments to each other.

"She didn't have very much stuff, did she?" said Olivia. "I haven't noticed any personal mementos, family pictures, that kind of thing."

"No, except for this picture on the nightstand. I'm betting it's her ex. He's nice looking," commented Annabelle. She was sitting on the bed, emptying the drawer of the nightstand. "Not much here; tissues, aspirin, some bobby pins, a little hard candy."

In the kitchen, the three had almost finished packing up any food. Because it was a furnished cabin most of the kitchen supplies stayed where they were.

Wanda was opening the last of the cabinets. "Oh, look. Here are all those natural supplements she was taking. Let's see, fish oil, garlic, glucosamine, and here's green tea, of course. I even drink that myself. What's this? She's got four bottles of it, 'extract of bitter orange.' Have you ever heard of that?"

The other two shook their heads and moved over to look more closely. "Never heard of it. We need to get Tessa or Olivia here to look it up on their iPhones."

Tessa came into the kitchen, pulling the phone from her pocket. "I heard my services are needed," she said. "What do you want me to google?"

"It's this supplement," said Kay, showing her the round bottle of tablets. "We've never heard of it. Can you find out about it?"

"Sure. No problem." Tessa used her thumbs to fly over the keypad as the others gathered around.

"Here it is. Listen to this. 'The extract of bitter orange has been marketed as a dietary supplement purported to act as a weight-loss aid and appetite suppressant. Bitter orange contains the tyramine metabolites N-Methyltrymine, octopamine and synephrine, substances similar to epinephrine, which act on the adrenergic receptor to constrict blood vessels and increase blood pressure and heart rate.' She must have been taking these for dieting."

"But that epinephrine can be bad stuff. I had it once at the dentist, and I thought I was having a heart attack," said Wanda.

"Oh, my gosh, listen to this," Tessa continued reading, "It's got a form of ephedra, and it lists all these bad side effects. Then it says, 'potential side effects include irregular heartbeat, seizures, heart attack, stroke, and death.' Maybe one of those things happened to her when she was walking around the lake and she fell in and drowned." The friends looked at each other, wide-eyed and speculating.

"Could that be possible?" asked Kay.

"Do you think Officer Barta saw this? I wonder if she was tested for this when they did the toxicology test," said Roberta.

Annabelle shook her head. "No, I bet Officer Barta assumed these were simply another supplement. With the toxicology tests they're not testing for everything possible. They're looking for illegal drugs or alcohol, things like that."

"I think we should take these right to the police," said Myra.

Annabelle nodded, "But I think we should give them to Martha and have her contact Officer Barta. That would be the best way."

"Agreed," said Roberta. "Let's finish packing everything up so we can get back to Myra's. This might put a whole new spin on what happened to Bev."

Two hours later Martha and Hank Myers returned from browsing the shops in Angel Fire. Their bags showed they had made purchases at Alpine Gifts and the Sweet Shirt Company.

"I'm glad to see you're supporting the local economy," said Myra with a smile on her face.

Hank chuckled. "Martha always likes to support any local economy wherever we are."

Martha swatted his shoulder. "I was trying to keep my mind off what Myra and her friends were doing. I kept picturing that empty cabin. All my sister's things. It's breaking my heart."

"I know this is a hard time for you," said Myra as Hank shuffled off to the downstairs apartment. "I have all the boxes in the garage. Why don't I fix us each a cup of tea and we'll sit on the deck for a while? I have some oatmeal raisin cookies that would taste good right now."

Martha gave a wan smile and followed Myra into the kitchen. Myra bustled about, filling the tea kettle with water, turning the fire on under it and setting out two cups on a tray with the plate of cookies. "There's something very soothing about making tea, don't you think?" Myra asked as she put tea bags in the china tea pot.

"I just put a cup of water and a tea bag in the microwave back at our trailer. We don't go in for fancy very much."

"Well, you relax and we'll have a nice visit. There are a few things I'd like to ask you about."

They perched on the chairs on either side of the glass table on the deck and stirred their tea. Myra offered the plate of cookies to Martha, picked up a cookie for herself and set it on the napkin beside her cup. "I mentioned to you that these friends of mine are very good at solving puzzles. I think we can help figure out what happened to your sister. We're interested in learning more about that foster brother you mentioned, Zack."

"Oh, that Zack Sadowsky, he was a mean one. He was so big, and Bev was so small, I mean petite. He'd only do things when the foster parents weren't around. Things like punch her in the stomach, or trip her when she walked by him. Of course, we tried to keep away from him. He did mean things, too. He'd tear up her homework, or make her bike tires flat."

"This is hard to ask, but was he also sexually abusive toward Bev?"

Martha face flushed. "I....I don't really know. Maybe in those years after I left that foster home. I wouldn't put it past him, he was so awful. He did expose himself to us many times, but we ignored him." She paused. "I think there was something wrong with him that way, you know? Like there was something dark and evil in him. I shouldn't say those things about someone else. I don't really know. It's a feeling I've always had about him."

"Do you think they still kept in contact with each other?" asked Myra.

"I can't imagine that Bev would have anything to do with him. She wanted to be rid of him forever. She used to talk about ways to get back at him, but she never acted on any of them. I think he tried to contact her a few times over the years."

"Did he want to get together with her or something?"

Martha shrugged her shoulders. "Who knows? The last time was maybe two or three years ago. He called me, too. He had had a heart attack and couldn't work in construction anymore. I think he was calling everyone he ever knew looking for a handout or something. Neither one of us would give him the time of day."

"Did you know he is in Taos? One of my friends found out on the Internet," said Myra. She noted the startled expression on Martha's face upon hearing that news.

"Taos! Oh my God, do you suppose he knew she was here so close?" Her expression became more alarmed. "You don't think he...Oh, Lordy. Do you think he did something to her?"

"I don't know, but I believe you should give Officer Barta that information and tell him all you told me about Zack." Myra munched on her cookie, giving Martha time to process that disturbing revelation.

They sat in silence for a few moments. A Red-tailed Hawk soared above the trees. Myra watched until it disappeared from view, and then asked, "Was Bev dieting?"

"Bev was always dieting, off and on. She was short and small-boned, but she did put on weight easily. I know she'd been dieting during that time she thought she might get Mike to come back to her. She was always trying some new diet."

"We found a supply of something called 'extract of bitter orange'. It was in with all her supplements. It's often used as a weight-loss aid."

"I've never heard of it, and Bev hadn't mentioned it to me. She'd read about all these nature things you can get on line and send for them."

"This bitter orange thing had ephedra in it. It can have serious side effects."

"Like what?" asked Martha.

"Like a racing heartbeat, maybe stroke, heart attack, or even death."

Martha's eyes filled with tears. "First, you make me think Zack murdered her, and now you suggest she took too much of that stuff and had a heart attack or something. I don't know what to think!"

Myra patted Martha's arm. "It's a lot to take in all at once, I know. All these ideas of possibilities that my friends and I have discovered should be passed on to Officer Barta. He can order tests to either confirm or rule out whether or not Bev had ephedra in her system. But the tests have already shown that drowning was the cause of death. So, the real question is, how did she get to the lake? And why? The more we can learn about Bev and what was happening in her life then, the better we can help figure out what really happened."

That evening, Kay and Ben sat on the deck of the country club lounge enjoying the night air while Jeremy was watching the Movie Under the Stars in the front of the clubhouse. Kay wore a red sweater over her red and white striped shell and white slacks. Ben commented on how attractive the color red was on her, and she was reminded of how long it had been since a man had given her a compliment, and how much she liked it. When their server, Bill, brought their glasses of wine, Ben lifted his toward Kay. "Here's to hoping Jeremy can get his life together."

"I'll drink to that," said Kay as they clinked their glasses lightly together. After taking a sip, Kay set her drink down. "What a strange set of circumstances it was that brought you and Jeremy together. You've been wonderful for him. I can't imagine anyone else doing what you're doing, nor what would have happened to that boy if things had been different. What if I'd called the police right away, or if he'd run off? And, even more important, what if you hadn't been the one to see him at my house that day." Ben smiled at her.

"Strange circumstances, coincidence, or God's hand – that's the million dollar question, isn't it?" replied Ben.

"I believe it was God's hand. Surely you, as a minister do too, don't you?"

"I do see God's hand everywhere in many different ways. I believe God gives us gifts and abilities to use to do his work. Do I believe that God's will is in everything? Probably not. I don't believe, for example, that he gave my lovely wife cancer. Life happens. But I do believe he is with us every step of the way through that life to help us find within ourselves the strengths that we need." Ben chuckled. "Remember, I'm a Methodist. There's a wide range of beliefs in Methodism."

Kay smiled at him. "There's a wide range of beliefs throughout Christianity, isn't there? I guess that means there's a place for both of us." She paused a moment. "I'm glad you took Jeremy to talk to the police. Do you think that information will amount to anything?"

"Honestly? No, and I'm not sure it helped Jeremy any in looking like a good citizen. Officer Barta probably had already checked out the possibility of a drifter using that cabin, and they were long gone so it was a cold lead. I had the feeling that he didn't think much of Jeremy. Just between us, my opinion of Officer Barta is that he is young and inexperienced and he wants to declare this an accident and move on to something with a little more substance."

Kay frowned. "I hate to hear that."

"The thing I think might be an important piece of information is the driver that gave Jeremy a ride from Taos to Angel Fire. It was interesting that he obviously was lying about why he was coming here. Why would he do that? It's important, I think, because that's about the time of the woman's death."

"You're starting to think like the Snoop Sisters," Kay said, her smile lighting up her face.

"The Snoop Sisters?"

"Yes, that's the name we, at our breakfast group, gave ourselves since we're so good at figuring out mysteries. We hope to discover what happened to Bev Tensley, the woman in the lake."

Ben shook his head. "You are a person of many talents."

They leaned back and looked to the night sky. The blanket of stars was beginning to form a covering over the valley, the moon rising above the mountain. The wind rustled gently through the trees with its soft, soothing song. Kay was reminded of a poem her mother used to say to her when she was little. She whispered the ending, "'God's in his heaven. All's right with the world.'"

"Amen," said Ben, smiling at her.

CHAPTER FOURTEEN

Finally, after an arduous day with the climb then a pizza dinner, Ted had taken the boys to the country club for the outdoor movie. They each had a warm comforter in case the night turned chilly, and they had Mindy's cell phone to call when it was time to be picked up.

Roberta, Al, and Mindy were waiting on the deck when Ted returned. Al held up his beer. "Can I get you one, or do you want a glass of wine?"

"Neither, thanks. I just want to get this off my chest, and see what you think I should do." Ted looked around at each of them as they sat silent and waiting. He pulled up a chair and sat facing them.

"Well, there's no easy way to say this, so I'll simply put it out there. You know I have a gambling addiction. It started when I was in college, and I've struggled to keep it under control. Obviously, I failed at that and I'm sorry, sorrier than I can ever express." He looked at Mindy, whose eyes shone with unshed tears. Ted gripped his hands together as he leaned forward.

"I'm so thankful that you're giving me this chance to put our family back together. That's all I want, and I'll do anything to accomplish that."

Roberta and Al sat silently listening, and Roberta realized she'd been holding her breath. She took a deep breath and nodded at Ted.

"This last year and a half were the worst it's ever been. I was spending a lot of time at the casinos, time I should have been with my family, or at work. I pray that with the counseling, I'll never get myself in that position again."

Mindy wiped a tear that had escaped and was sliding down her cheek.

Ted cleared his throat. "But, because of what I was doing, there is a real problem now." He jumped up and paced to the deck railing and back. He dropped back into his chair. "When we were up here last April, I ran into someone I knew from the casino, a dealer. Back in April you didn't know yet about the gambling, remember?" he said, looking directly at Mindy. She nodded.

"I was so afraid that person would say something, and then it would all come out. I found out where she was living up here and that evening I . . . I went to see her. I told her that my family didn't know about my gambling and begged her not to say anything. I thought she might demand some money, like blackmail or something, but she didn't. She said she wouldn't say anything. I was so relieved. I left her cabin and drove to the lake and sat there for a little while, then drove around thinking, wishing I could get my life together, wondering how I could possibly come up with the money for my gambling debts."

"So that's where you went that evening," said Mindy.

Ted nodded.

"Is that what you needed to tell us?" asked Roberta, her voice reflecting her puzzlement.

"That's not quite all. It's what I've learned since then. The person's name was Bev Tensley, the woman who was found drowned in the lake that night."

The stunned silence reverberated around them for a moment. Roberta felt as though she had been struck across the chest and all the wind had been knocked out of her. Mindy's hands had flown to her mouth and her eyes reflected the depth of her emotions.

Al shook his head. "Oh, my God, Ted. You could be a suspect for her murder if they decide she was murdered."

Ted began to pace again. "I know. I know. I don't know what to do. Should I go to the police and tell them what I know? But if I do, will they arrest me as a suspect? Maybe they've found my fingerprints or something at her cabin."

"You'll have to go to them, Ted," said Roberta. "You need to tell them when you saw her alive. Maybe you were the last person to see her before she died. How did she seem?"

"How did she seem? I don't know. She was surprised to see me. She acted kind of distracted, like she had something else on her mind."

"Was anyone else around?" Al asked. "A witness?"

Ted shook his head. "No. I didn't see anyone. There were people over at the RV park area, but that's a little distance from where her cabin is." He paused. "Now that I think of it, there was a pickup truck turning into her drive as I came out. He had to wait as I pulled out before he turned in."

"Ted, that could be important information for the police. You have to go to them and tell everything you know," Roberta said.

Al kept shaking his head, trying to absorb the implications of what Ted told them. "You know the woman, you went to see her that night, and you were at the lake. My God, Ted! All you need is a witness seeing you push her in the lake. Did you see anyone else at the lake?"

"No. There wasn't anyone at the lake. I sat in my car there for a little while, and then kept driving."

Ted dropped into his chair and took Mindy's hand. "What do you think? What should I do, Mindy?"

Her voice trembled as she spoke. "I don't think you have a choice. You have to go to the police, Ted."

On the Monday morning Trekkers hike on the Oeste Vista Trail, Tessa was glad to see Ben had joined them, and he was by himself without the boy. Tessa had noticed that whenever Ben and Jeremy were together in a crowd, Jeremy would stick closely to Ben's side. Although this morning had the usual sized group, perhaps she and Jim would get a chance to talk to Ben about being foster parents.

This was a favorite hike of Tessa's. She pushed herself up the long, uphill climb as they started. At the 90 degree turn she always liked to pause and view the scene across the valley of the mountains to the west. It was a popular stopping place with the wooden table and benches placed there beside the trail. Because Ben was at the tables, Tessa took advantage of the opportunity. "Ben, could Jim and I talk to you a minute?" she asked.

"Sure," he responded, sitting on the bench. "I don't mind a little break."

Jim began, "We're thinking of applying to become foster parents. Kay said you and your wife had done a lot of that. We're looking for some insights or advice, I guess."

"That's wonderful!" said Ben. "We need good foster parents so badly, not only in New Mexico, but in every state."

"We can talk as we hike," said Tessa.

Ben smiled. "OK, but if I get too winded to talk, let's stop again. This altitude, you know, and I'm getting older."

"You set the pace," Jim said as they started off again.

"What age child or children were you thinking about?" asked Ben.

Tessa and Jim glanced at each other. "We haven't really decided," Jim began, "but I don't think it would be teenagers. That's a little too challenging for us."

"Or babies," added Tessa. "That's challenging, too, but I guess it could be a possibility."

"That leaves a good range. My wife and I had only teens, and usually troubled teens." Ben chuckled. "Not that there's any other kind, but the ones we had were more troubled than most."

"How did you handle that?" asked Jim.

"It was rarely easy. My wife was especially good with them. She had a blend of firmness and unconditional love that was so necessary. I'll be honest with you. Being a foster parent isn't easy. If a kid is in foster care, it's obvious he or she comes with a lot of baggage. I mean that figuratively. Literally, they come with almost nothing. Of course, you get some financial help, but you'll find you also use your own money a lot to help these kids fit in with their peers as far as clothes and school trips. Things like that."

Tessa nodded. "We could do that. I think what worries me the most is having a child for a while, then having her – or him – move on, either back to their own family or to some other foster home."

"That's one of the hard things," said Ben. "You do get attached to these kids. Of course, the goal is to get them returned to their family, but so often, even if things have improved it's probably only temporary. That means more unsettling for the kids. It breaks your heart, for sure. Then, too, there are times you're glad a kid moves on. We hate to admit it, but it's true. Being a foster parent can be frustrating, demanding, exhausting, making you wish you'd never signed on. But, the important thing is it is one of the most fulfilling, rewarding things my wife and I have ever done, and I wouldn't trade the experience for anything. Making a difference in a child's life is a tremendous blessing."

Jim took Tessa hand and squeezed it. "Those have been our thoughts, too." he said.

Ted had arranged to stay another day in Angel Fire, and now he waited nervously for Officer Barta to meet with him. He was glad his in-laws had suggested meeting at their house. Al had taken the boys to Red River for the day, but Mindy and Roberta would be with him. He knew he didn't deserve their support, but he was extremely thankful for it. When he tried to express that to Roberta, she cut him off.

"We are supportive for Mindy and the boys' sake, Ted. We do not condone anything you have done. We do hope you all can be a family again for their sake."

Ted held his hands up in resignation. "I know. Believe me, I know and understand."

At that moment the doorbell rang, ending any conversation. Roberta answered the door and brought Officer Barta into the room. "Please, have a seat," she said. Mindy and Roberta sat on the sofa, and Officer Barta took a seat in a side chair. He pulled out his notebook and pen and looked expectantly at Ted.

Ted remained standing. He clasped his hands together and began. "Thank you for taking the time to see me. I'm not sure where to start, but I thought that what I know may be of some interest to you in the case of the woman you found in the lake, Bev Tensley."

He paused and cleared his throat. "I....I knew her in Albuquerque. She was a dealer at a casino I went to...often. Uh, at that time, my wife didn't know the extent of my gambling, and I didn't want her to know." He glanced at Mindy, anguish showing in his expression. "We, that is my wife and our two boys, had come up here to Angel Fire that weekend."

Officer Barta interrupted. "What weekend was that?"

"Oh, sorry, I should have said. That was the weekend of April 17th. I remember because it was right after we'd done our taxes."

Officer Barta jotted a few notes down, and looked at Ted to continue.

"We had come up that morning. I took the day off. So, anyway, we all went out for lunch at Zeb's. We were about halfway through our meal when I saw Bev at the bar. I was so afraid she'd come over and greet me or something. I excused myself from the table, said I wanted to get a beer. I went up to Bev and quickly asked her not to act like she knew me. I said I wanted to talk to her and asked to meet her later."

"Why did you want to meet with her? Couldn't you simply ask her not to reveal she knew you?" said the officer.

"Well, I wanted to make sure she wouldn't ever let on how much I was at the casino. She said I could come by her cabin that evening if it was early. She told me where she lived."

"Did she say why she wanted you to come early?"

"No. I assumed she had a date or something."

"And did you go to her cabin?"

Ted swallowed hard, sighed, and answered. "Yes."

"What time did you get there?"

"It was before dinner. I guess around 5:30 or 6 p.m."

"So you went to the victim's cabin around 5:30 or 6 on the night she went missing?" He unconsciously scratched the side of his head with the pen.

"I….Well, I….Yes. Yes, I went there, but she was perfectly fine when I left. I only stayed a few minutes." Ted's glance flew between his wife and his questioner. "I was afraid to come to you with this information because you might consider me a suspect if it turns out to be a murder. But, I only went there to talk for a few minutes then I left. I thought you might need to know that she was still alive at that time."

Officer Barta stared at Ted a moment before he asked, "What did you talk about in those few minutes?"

Ted slipped into a nearby chair as if his legs would no longer hold him up. "I thanked her for not saying anything to me at lunch. I told her that my gambling was causing a big problem in my life, that my debts were piling up, and I didn't want my wife to know how bad it was. I begged her not to say anything if she saw us again or if she ever saw my in-laws, since they live here."

"And what did she say?"

"She told me to stop gambling, and she said my secret was safe with her."

"Did she act as if she was anxious for you to leave, as if she was expecting someone else?"

Ted thought for a moment, and then shook his head. "Not really. She did act a little distracted, as though her mind was someplace else. Our conversation was very brief. I thanked her then left."

"Did anyone see you leave?" Officer Barta asked.

Again, Ted shook his head. "No." He paused. "Well, as I was pulling out, someone in a pickup was waiting to turn into her driveway, but I have no idea who he was or if he noticed any more than the fact that a car was pulling out."

Officer Barta continued making notes. Without looking up, he asked, "What color was the pickup?"

"It was red. One of those raised up pickups. That's all I noticed."

"What did you do after you left there?"

"I drove around for a while, first to Monte Verde Lake, then on out Route 434. I like that road to Ocate. There's a place right at a turn where you can pull off and look out over the valley. A good place to think, you know?"

"So, when did you return to where you were staying that weekend?"

"We stayed here with my in-laws. It was a bad time for me with my gambling and all and I needed to get myself together so I sat there quite a while. I guess I got back about 8 p.m."

Officer Barta looked at Mindy and Roberta. "Do you remember that evening? Was that the time he returned?"

They both nodded yes. Roberta's throat was so dry she didn't think she could have spoken, and, evidently, Mindy's was the same.

"That's an awfully long time to be driving around or sitting in a car somewhere," was Officer Barta's comment.

Ted simply shrugged.

The questioning continued. "Did you go back to the lake?"

Ted shook his head.

"When you passed the lake on your return to your in-laws did you see Mrs. Tensley or anything suspicious?"

"I didn't go back to the lake. I came here from that place I like to pull over. I didn't notice anything at the lake at all. I don't think I even glanced that way."

"Is there anything else you want to say?"

Ted stood and paced a few steps. "No. I thought this might be of help in some way, that's all."

Officer Barta stood and closed his notebook. "Oh, it's been of much interest. I'll need your number in case I need to contact you again. I suggest you don't leave the state."

Ted pulled out one of his cards from his pocket. "I thought you might want this, and, no, I don't plan to leave the state."

Roberta rose and said, "I'll show you out." As they left the room, Officer Barta turned and gave Ted a last long look. As if Ted wasn't apprehensive enough, that look made him even more so.

It was turning into a busy day for Officer Barta. After talking with Ted at the Streit's home, he drove to Mrs. Stanhope's home to hear what the victim's sister had to tell him. He had had a message from her on his answering machine Saturday afternoon. Judging from her tone of voice, she might have something interesting for him. He was not anxious to see Mrs. Stanhope, though. He considered her to be the ultimate busybody. She had no business sticking her nose in this investigation. However, with Martha and Hank Myers staying in the Stanhope home, he knew he would probably have to endure seeing Myra Stanhope, too.

While driving, he mulled over the direction the case was taking. He had hoped it would only be that Bev Tensley was walking around the lake that evening and somehow stumbled into the water. The water was very cold still in April, and this year the water level was unusually high. In fact, he had learned that the canoes and boats, which had been pulled onto the land at the end of the season, were covered with water and had floated out into the lake because of all the rain in Angel Fire at that time. Perhaps because the ground was soggy, she had lost her footing, fallen in the lake, suffered from hypothermia and drowned. A simple explanation.

Yet, here were all these locals complicating everything. This was looking more and more like a murder. First, there was the possibility of a drifter being in town at that particular time and perhaps doing something to the victim. Maybe he tried to get money from her while she was out walking and, in a struggle, he pushed her into the lake and she drowned. But, how would he ever get any evidence for that scenario?

Then there was that boy, Jeremy Townson. If ever there was a likely suspect it was Jeremy. He had a shady past, no upbringing, obviously. Just because that minister is standing up for him doesn't mean he isn't guilty. He could easily have broken into her cabin and tried to steal from her. Considering the distance to her cabin, though, it was perhaps more logical that he was the one who accosted her while she walked around the lake. But why in the world would someone be walking there at that time in April when their cabin was such a distance from the lake?

No, the most likely scenario at this point was this guy, Ted Gilmore. He had motive and opportunity. He didn't seem like the kind of person to commit a murder, though. Still he was the number one suspect at this point.

Officer Barta sifted through all the facts again. He hadn't heard back from his contact in Albuquerque yet who was checking out the ex-husband, Mike Tensley. As he pulled into Mrs. Stanhope's driveway, he made a mental note to push for the information on the ex-husband.

CHAPTER FIFTEEN

Myra ushered Officer Barta into the living room where Martha and Hank Myers waited. She offered him coffee, which he declined, but he did look appreciatively at the plate of cranberry muffins.

"Maybe later," he replied when Myra offered him a muffin, as he took out his notebook and pen and sat in a chair opposite the Myers. They already had cups of coffee in front of them, as did Myra, but no one had started on the muffins.

Martha leaned forward. "What have you learned about my sister's death?" she asked, her voice carrying the concern she was feeling.

"We're making progress, even though it is difficult with the lapse of time since her death." He lifted his pen to scratch the side of his head. "As I told you when we first talked, we know the cause of death was drowning. Additionally, there had been a blow to the head, either by striking something in a fall, or by some kind of blunt instrument." He looked around at Myra, then back at Martha. "I have to ask, Mrs. Myers, since this is an ongoing investigation, do you want an outsider to be privy to our conversation?"

Myra drew back as if she had been insulted but managed to stay silent while Martha answered.

"I do not consider Myra Stanhope an outsider." Her irritation at the implication definitely showed in her expression and in the tone of her voice. "Myra has done more for us, more for me, than anyone else. I not only have no problem with her being here, but I would expect and want her to be here."

Myra couldn't help but let a little smile out as she met Martha's glance and a little nod toward Officer Barta as if to say 'So there!"

Officer Barta sighed and looked back at his notebook. "We are still considering three possible causes of your sister's death - an accident, suicide, or murder."

He looked up at Martha and continued. "There are leads for all three. It's possible that she accidently fell in the lake and drowned while walking around it. It's also possible that from what we have learned about her disappointment at learning of her ex-husband's new family, she might have committed suicide. And murder remains the third possibility."

"Which of the three do you suspect?" asked Hank.

"I am sorry to tell you this, as I know it's disturbing, but I am beginning to believe that your sister was murdered."

Martha bit her lower lip to try and hold back the tears that were in her eyes.

"But you said you have some information for me, Mrs. Myers. That may change everything, so please, what did you think of to tell me?"

Martha took a deep breath. "There are two things, Officer, which I have recently learned. One is that a foster brother we lived with for several years when we were in the last foster home, a person who, I believe, is twisted in some evil way, is now living in Taos. He was extremely abusive to Bev throughout those years. She always wanted to get back at him, but never did. I can't help but wonder if they somehow got together, and that was part of the picture of what happened to her."

"It is a possibility we need to investigate," said Officer Barta, nodding. "What is his name, and do you have his address in Taos?"

"His name is Zack Sadowsky." Her glance swept over to Myra. "I don't know his exact address."

Noticing the look exchanged between the two women, Officer Barta asked, "Do you know this person, Mrs. Stanhope?"

"Me? No, I don't know him."

"Why did Mrs. Myers look to you as if you might know his address?"

Myra shifted in her seat slightly. "It's just that when Martha told us about him, and about his behavior, well, we thought we should learn about him and where he lived and all."

"And who is this 'we' you're talking about?"

"You know. The group of us that has breakfast together every Tuesday. We're the ones that found out where those mountain bikers had been stashed." She fingered the fabric of her slacks, trying to keep her hands from shaking.

Officer Barta slapped the notebook against his leg. "Good Lord, Mrs. Stanhope! What do you think you're doing, interfering with a police investigation?"

Myra's eyes blazed. "We're not interfering in any way. We're helping you. You should be glad of our help."

"Well, surprise. I'm not glad. It could be very dangerous for you if this was a murder. How do you know the murderer won't find out about your meddling and try to do away with you?"

Martha put her arm out toward both of them. "Please. Stop. This is my sister we're talking about. My sister's life. I want you to do whatever it takes to find out what happened to Bev, and if it was a murder, to bring the murderer to justice. Please, Officer Barta. Please take this information in the spirit it was offered to help you solve Bev's case."

Officer Barta sat back and nodded. "Of course, Mrs. Myers. That is exactly what we want to do." He paused. "Now, you said there were two things. What was the other?"

"I don't know if the second is important. When going through my sister's things at the cabin, we found this diet supplement she was using." Martha deliberately didn't look at Myra when she mentioned going through the cabin. "I know it contains ephedra, which could have caused a heart attack, stroke, or death. Can you still test to see if this was in her system, and to see if it might have had anything to do with her death?" She handed him the bottle of bitter orange that had been in her pocket.

Taking the bottle, he studied it for a moment and slipped it into his pocket. "I'll see what we can do. Was that everything you've thought of that might be helpful?"

Martha nodded. "Yes, that's all for now."

Officer Barta stood up and put away his notebook and pen. "Thank you for this information. I'll process it and get back to you if we learn that it is relevant." He started to leave, looking at the plate of muffins as he stepped around the coffee table.

Myra picked up the plate and held it toward him. "Please, Officer Barta, take one to eat on your way." She was secretly proud of herself for letting her sense of hospitality overcome her real feelings.

With only a fraction of a second's hesitancy, he picked up a muffin. "Thank you, Mrs. Stanhope. I appreciate it."

She followed him to the hallway and opened the door as he put his hat on. He turned to her and said, "Please be careful, ma'am. Just be careful."

She smiled and nodded at him, shutting the door gently behind him.

Office Barta went directly to the Angel Fire Police office. Sitting with Chief McCaslin in his office, Officer Barta went over all the details of the case with the chief. He flipped through his notebook, mentioning all the items of information he had collected.

"I hate to say anything against one of your residents," he began, "but that Mrs. Stanhope is driving me crazy."

"Sounds to me like she's being a helpful citizen," the chief replied, trying not to smile.

"But the audacity of that woman to think she and a bunch of old ladies could solve a murder case! They have no business getting involved. Besides, it could be dangerous for them, or worse than that, they could completely mess up our investigation."

"I've been in this business a lot longer than you, Andy. Let me give you a little advice. Learn to work with the community."

"It's one thing to work with the community," he replied. "It's quite another to have this woman calling you all the time thinking she's giving you clues."

The chief chuckled. "I understand how you feel. This is your first investigation, and it's turning out to be an important one. One that is very complicated. I'm just saying, take help from wherever you can get it. And, by the way, they're not that old."

"I need to call Albuquerque and see what they found out talking to the ex-husband. Mind if I use your phone?"

"Go right ahead. And you might ask them what kind of vehicle that guy drives. Be interesting if it's a raised red and silver Ford 150 pickup, wouldn't it?"

Officer Barta leaned back and sighed deeply. "I thought this was a simple accidental drowning. Now I've got more possibilities than I want." He shook his head and reached for the phone on the chief's desk.

When Al got home with the boys later Monday afternoon, he and Roberta slipped back into their bedroom.

"Well, what happened?" he asked anxiously.

Roberta sat on the edge of the bed. "Ted told them everything, like he had told us. That state trooper asked him lots of questions, pinpointing time and exactly what Ted had done."

"Do you think the officer believed him?"

"I don't know. He's very young, but he seemed to know what to ask to get all the facts. I had this uneasy feeling that he wasn't seeing Ted the way we know him, but as someone who might have done some harm to Bev. Honestly, I don't know."

Al strode back and forth. "What a mess. How could Ted have turned out to be someone to cause this family so much trouble? Only a few months ago, I thought we were all fine, everybody was OK. Our four kids and their families were happy and healthy. We didn't have a care in the world. And now look at us! Mindy's family is broken and we're facing a son-in-law being arrested as a suspect in a murder."

Roberta's eyes filled with tears. "I know. But let's not look at the worst side of all this. Ted and Mindy are working at reconciliation. We don't even know if this was a murder. It might have been suicide or an accident. Even if it turns out to be a murder, there are other suspects."

Al stopped in his tracks and turned to Roberta. "How do you know that, Bertie? I told you not to get involved, didn't I? Have you and your friends been getting into this business?"

Roberta felt her ire rising up. "In the first place, we don't have the kind of marriage where you tell me what I can and cannot do. In the second place, you know that Bev's sister, Martha, is staying at Myra's, so of course, we're hearing all the details of the case." She glared at Al.

He paused and came and sat by her side. His shoulders slumped. "You're right, hon. I am so stressed about all this it's making me crazy."

Roberta's expression softened. "I know. It's making me crazy, too. But we can't let all this get to us so much that we fuss between us."

Al took her hand in his. "Right," he said and kissed her cheek. "How was your day with the boys?" she asked, more than ready to change the subject.

As Al gave a detailed account of all they had done in Red River, Roberta let her mind wander. *How quickly life can change,* she thought. The line from a poem she had learned in high school flashed through her mind; *Gather ye rosebuds while ye may.* Life was truly full of uncertainties. She wondered if Wanda had a tee shirt for that.

Officer Barta spent the time driving back to the state police headquarters evaluating all the information he had. According to his call to Albuquerque, the investigator there had gone by the ex-husband, Mike Tensley's, house, and it was the first Tensley had heard that his ex-wife had died. The investigating officer said that Tensley seemed genuinely shocked. After checking his calendar, Tensley had stated that he probably spent the evening watching television on April 17th, but he did not have an alibi for the time of Bev Tensley's death because his present wife was out of town so he was alone at home.

Before pulling into the office, Andy Barta realized that he hadn't had anything to eat except that muffin since breakfast so he went through the KFC drive through and got a chicken sandwich and a large Pepsi. Back at his own desk, he dropped his hat in an empty chair, plopped in his own swivel chair and opened up the KFC bag. His glance rested on a blue memo on the corner of the desk. He slid it towards him and read the message.

He dropped the chicken sandwich back on the paper it had come in and reread the information. *This Zack Sadowsky is one bad dude,* he thought. The memo showed a long arrest history for assault, mostly on women. He noted the address where Sadowsky lived and decided to head over there as soon as he'd finished his sandwich.

Half an hour later, he arrived at his destination, an old, dilapidated trailer out Route 64 towards the Gorge Bridge. Zack Sadowsky was sitting on the trailer steps, smoking. He remained seated, watching with a wary expression, as Officer Barta walked up. He was a large man, his brown hair long, and he sported a bushy mustache. He was wearing jeans and a white tee shirt, and he was barefooted.

After identifying himself, Officer Barta said, "Are you Zack Sadowsky?"

"That's me," was the abrupt reply.

"We're investigating the death of a Beverly Tensley in Angel Fire back in April," Officer Barta said. "Did you know her?"

"Who?"

"Beverly Tensley. Perhaps you knew her by her maiden name," Officer Barta said, checking his notes. "Beverly Bronner. You were both in a foster home together for several years."

"Oh, yeah. I 'member her. Cute little thing. So, she died? That's too bad."

"When was the last time you saw her?"

"So many years ago, I couldn't remember. I guess when I left that foster home. Probably twenty years ago."

"And you've never seen her since then?"

Zack shrugged. "Our paths may have crossed a time or two over the years. Can't really recollect."

"Where were you the night of April 17th?"

"I don't keep track of dates much. I guess I was working. I'm a bartender at the Good Times Bar here in Taos."

"That your vehicle?" Officer Barta asked, nodding at a beat up, faded blue pickup sitting nearby.

"Yup, and it's all registered and insured."

"Did you know Mrs. Tensley had been living in Angel Fire?"

"No kidding? Well, imagine that." He ground out his cigarette on the steps and stood up. "I got to get ready for work. You got any more questions for me?"

"Not right now. I'll be checking with your employer about whether or not you were there April 17th. Don't plan on going anywhere in case I need to talk to you again."

Zack gave a sardonic smile. "I'm not aiming to go anywhere." He turned and went into his trailer.

Officer Barta returned to his office. He sat back in his chair swiveling back and forth, his favorite thinking mode. He would check out Sadowsky's alibi. If he had not been working at the bar that night, he certainly could be a suspect if this was a murder. Officer Barta leaned his head back and sighed. Of course, so could Ted Gilmore and Jeremy Townson, or maybe even some homeless drifter who was long gone. And there's still a possibility it was an accident or suicide. *Why couldn't my first official case be some easy cut-and-dried thing?* he thought.

He reached for the pink telephone memo slip on top of the files on his desk and pulled it over. His eyes skimmed the message, and he bolted upright and grabbed up the phone. He punched in the number for Albuquerque, and drummed his fingers on the desk waiting for an answer.

Finally getting to the investigator who had interviewed Mike Tensley, he said, "Listen, that description of this guy's truck matches one seen going into Bev Tensley's driveway the night of her disappearance. Go ahead and pick him up for questioning. I'll be there in two and a half hours."

CHAPTER SIXTEEN

Officer Barta pushed open the door to the interrogation room. Mike Tensley sat leaning on the cold metal table, his head in his hands. He was dressed casually in jeans and a Lobos tee shirt. When the door closed, he looked up, his eyes red-rimmed with a tense, worried look.

Officer Barta identified himself, and slapped a manila file on the desk as he sat in the opposite chair. He pulled a small tape recorder from his pocket and set it on the table between them. "I will be recording our conversation," he said. "You don't have any objection, I assume?"

Mike shook his head.

"Mike Tensley, you are the ex-husband of Beverly Tensley, are you not?" Officer Barta began after he clicked on the machine.

"Yes," was the soft reply.

"Where were you on the night of April 17th?"

Mike Tensley sighed and ran his hand through his curly brown hair. "I…," he began, cleared his throat, and began again. "I was in Angel Fire and Eagle Nest."

"What time did you arrive in Angel Fire that day?"

Mike shrugged. "I don't know exactly. Maybe about one or two in the afternoon."

"What did you do when you got there?"

"I drove around for a while, drove out toward Black Lake then I drove to Eagle Nest."

"Why?"

"Why?" repeated Mike, his expression bleak. "That's a good question. Why did I ever think I could get Beverly to make any sense? Why did I believe she might finally leave me alone?"

"I suggest you start from the beginning and tell me why you went up there and what happened when you went to see your ex-wife. We have witnesses that put you there the evening she died. I think you need to tell me the whole story."

Mike nodded. "OK. OK. Beverly is – was – a very unbalanced individual. Our marriage was a mistake from the beginning. Soon after we were married the arguments started, and it wasn't long before she would get very physical against me during our arguments, shoving me, hitting me, throwing things at me. She'd be in my face, criticizing, yelling, and cursing from the minute I'd get home from work. I swear, I never hit her back. I wasn't raised that way. It's a humiliating thing for a man to have his wife beating on him. It made me so isolated. I mean, I hated talking to my parents or my sisters and my friends, so I would hardly be in touch with them. I tried to leave her so many times. She'd find me and beg me to come back, say she'd kill herself if I didn't return, promised it wouldn't happen again. But it always did. Finally, I couldn't take it anymore and I filed for divorce. She'd call me at all hours, stalked me. I took out a restraining order against her, but she didn't stop. I changed my phone number several times, moved a couple of times. I tried to go on with my life."

Mike stopped, shook his head.

"Would you like some water?" asked Officer Barta.

"No. I'm OK. It's just hard to talk about it. Anyway, I met a wonderful woman and we married. We're expecting a baby soon. Our life would be perfect except that Beverly kept calling me, texting me, messaging me on Facebook. Honestly, Officer, I began to fear for our lives, wondering if she'd come after me or my wife, or maybe even our child someday."

"Did she threaten you?"

"Not in so many words. But, finally, I don't know why, I decided to come up and confront her. Try to convince her that I had another life and she needed to move on with her life."

"How did you know where she lived?"

"Oh, that was no problem. She'd invited me to her cabin so many times, implying that we could have some romantic rendezvous there. She'd even sent me exact directions."

"What time was it when you went to her cabin on the 17th?"

"It was about six p.m. probably."

"You got up there about one p.m. Why didn't you go right over?"

Mike rubbed his hands together the placed his palms on the table. Looking directly at his questioner he said, "I had to get my nerve up. I hadn't actually seen or talked to her in person for a few years. Could I stand to be around her again? I sat at the Lucky Shoe and had a couple of beers."

"When you got to her cabin, what happened?"

"Well, she was very surprised to see me, for sure. She actually seemed very ill at ease, nervous, though she had no reason to be. I only wanted to talk, to tell her to leave us alone. She invited me in."

"Did you go into her cabin?"

"Yes, I stepped inside, but I didn't go sit down or anything. I stayed near the door. I told her why I had come. I said she needed to move on with her life, and that we would never be getting back together and she had to leave me and my family alone."

"What was her reaction to that?"

"Ha! You can imagine, can't you? She started sobbing, saying she would kill herself."

"Did you ever think she might actually commit suicide?"

"No way."

"OK, so then what happened?"

"We just went back and forth like that for a while. The same old thing. Finally, I said it was useless to talk anymore and I was leaving. Then she suddenly stopped crying and said maybe if I paid her some money she would leave me alone."

"How did you respond?"

"I told her she was crazy. She knew I didn't have any extra money, and with a baby coming I'd be even more strapped. My trying to talk sense to her was a stupid waste of time. I don't know why I even tried. I turned around and left."

"You left? Are you sure your argument didn't escalate into violence? She shoved you. You shoved her back, and she fell and hit her head?"

"No, nothing like that. I swear. But I thought the other officer told me she drowned in the lake. Did she die from a blow to her head?"

"Drowning was the actual cause of death, but she had evidence of a hard blow to her head, either from a fall or from someone striking her."

"Good Lord! I know it looks bad for me, but I swear I didn't hurt her. I didn't have anything to do with her death. Maybe she actually did commit suicide, go to the lake and throw herself in. Why would I jeopardize my wonderful life by doing something to Bev? That's crazy."

"Did you kill Beverly Tensley?" was the blunt question.

"No! I could never kill anyone!"

"Did you strike her then carry her to the lake and drown her?"

"How can you think that? I had nothing to do with Bev's death!"

"Did you ever wish she were dead?" asked Officer Barta.

"I often wished she would vanish and stop harassing me, but I would never kill her!" Mike's voice was becoming more and more desperate. "You have to believe me."

"You had motive and you made the opportunity. Seems pretty clear to me."

Officer Barta stood, went to the door and called in a policeman. The policeman stood behind Mike as Officer Barta charged Mike Tensley with the murder of Beverly Tensley and read him his rights. As the officer led Mike away, his hands cuffed, Mike turned to Officer Barta.

"This is all a mistake. I'm innocent! I'm innocent!"

Tuesday morning brought a sunny day with small puffs of clouds which could, amazingly, build up to become thunderheads in the afternoon, bringing an isolated mountain shower. As each of the JULIETs arrived they checked out Wanda's tee shirt message, which this morning declared, "I think my guardian angel drinks."

"We have a lot to report this morning," Myra said. "Martha passed the bitter orange to the officer, and he said he would get it tested to see if Bev had that in her body. She also told him about the foster brother, and he indicated he'd look into that."

Roberta looked around at her friends wondering if she should share the news about Ted. As she hesitated, Kay began to tell about Jeremy's visit to the law enforcement officers.

"I wasn't there, of course, but Ben reported the conversation to me later. Ben wasn't sure the police thought Jeremy had any real information. I worry that they think he might have had something to do with Bev's death."

Olivia nodded. "I can see why they might consider him a suspect until they rule out that this was a murder."

Kay continued, "There was one thing Jeremy told them that Ben thinks might be an important fact. Of course, it could only be coincidence."

"What's that?" asked Annabelle.

"Well, the man that gave Jeremy a ride up here said he was going hiking here for a few days then fish in Eagle Nest for a few days. The strange thing was, he had nothing in the truck with him, no gear and no luggage."

"That is odd," said Wanda. "Do you think they'll try to find out who he was?"

"Maybe. I guess his truck was distinctive because Jeremy remembered it, a lifted red Ford 150 with silver trim."

Roberta set her cup down hard, spilling some of the hot coffee on her hand.

"Did you burn yourself?" asked Kay, handing her a wad of napkins.

"No. It's OK." She dapped up the spilled coffee. "The thing is, I need to tell you all something, but I'm asking you to keep this entirely confidential."

She paused and looked for their agreement. Once they had all nodded, she began.

"This is so distressing to our family that I hate to share it, but it might be important. Ted asked to talk to us Saturday. He told us that he knew Bev from the casino in Albuquerque. When they were up here in April he saw her. He was afraid she would say something. At that time he was still trying to keep his gambling a secret. He arranged to go see Bev that evening. He was going to beg her never to reveal how often he was at the casino." Again, she paused. "It was the evening of April 17th."

A collective gasp came from the group.

Roberta nodded, acknowledging their shock. "Exactly. So, if it is a murder, Ted becomes a prime suspect." Her voice faltered then she continued. "He asked us what he should do. Should he go to the police? We told him that he had to go. I mean, what if they eventually found fingerprints or a witness or something? We thought the police would be glad to know the time Bev was still alive." Roberta stopped, clasped her hands to stop their trembling, and shook her head.

She looked up again. "But this is why I told you all. Mindy and I were with him when Officer Barta questioned him. When he asked Ted if there were any witnesses to the time he left Bev's, first he said no. Then he remembered a truck was waiting to turn in Bev's drive as he was coming out. It was a lifted red truck."

"Wow!" Myra leaned toward Roberta. "I know that was hard for you to share, but that is very important. If this was a murder, and I'm beginning to think it might have been, then whoever brought Jeremy to Angel Fire could have been the murderer. We need to get that information to Officer Barta. Maybe that truck is Zack Sadowsky's. I wonder if we should go to Taos and check it out."

"Whoa, Myra," said Annabelle. "Think about it. Officer Barta already has this information. He questioned Jeremy and Ted, and didn't he tell Martha he would go question Zack? I imagine he's already trying to find out whose truck it is."

Frowning, Myra looked around the table. "But maybe we should make sure."

"I agree with Annabelle. Maybe later today Martha could call to see if there's been any progress on the case," suggested Olivia.

"I suppose that would work," said Myra.

"I have an idea," said Wanda. "Let's try to analyze the case. What are the possibilities of each of the three; suicide, accident, or murder? Myra, why don't you make a list?"

Myra clicked open her pen and turned to a blank page of the notebook. "OK. Let's start with accident. I think that's the most unlikely."

"To be an accident, she would have to have been walking around Monte Verde Lake at night in April, when it was still cold. Not very likely," said Olivia.

Roberta nodded. "Especially with the rain we had in April. Remember, the lake was flooded over the banks then. Don't forget how far she lives from the lake, too."

Myra put an "x" by "accident." "OK, what about suicide?"

"She was depressed about her ex and his new wife expecting a baby," mentioned Tessa.

Myra added, "And Martha said she was discouraged about finding a job up here. Martha said that Bev was tired of the casino scene and wanted to live up here, and that her savings were running out."

"But why would she go to the lake? And don't forget about the bump on her head. Wilda mentioned one time that she was enthusiastic about things up here, the hiking, and the plants, and all. That doesn't sound like someone who is so depressed they'd commit suicide," said Wanda.

"I agree," said Roberta. "Let's cross off suicide. I think this was a murder." She looked around at the group.

Myra put her pen next to the word "suicide." "All in favor of crossing out suicide?"

Each either nodded or raised a hand.

"I can't believe we're voting about a murder," muttered Kay.

"Now we have to think about how it happened and who the suspects are." Myra turned toward Roberta. "Not Ted, of course."

Roberta felt a chill go down her spine. It was unthinkable… wasn't it?

"If we knew who drove that red truck, we'd have the murderer," offered Tessa.

"I think it was either the ex-husband or that foster brother, Zack what's-his-name," said Olivia.

"I hope we're not going to vote on this," whispered Kay to Roberta.

Myra wrote the two names in the notebook. "OK, now, how did it happen?"

"Whichever one did it went to her cabin right after Ted. He pushed her around, and she fell and hit her head, then he took her to the lake and drowned her." Wanda sat back and looked to the others for agreement.

"So, was she unconscious from the blow to the head?" wondered Annabelle.

"Probably, or how else could he have gotten her there and drowned her?" asked Kay.

Annabelle smiled at her friends. "I think we've gotten very close to figuring out what happened to that poor woman. Now we have to wait and see what Officer Barta has come up with. If Martha learns anything, will you let us know, Myra?"

"Of course." Myra slowly put way the notebook as Annabelle continued.

"We haven't talked about a single thing besides this case today. Let's end on a more pleasant note. So, what about books, or grandchildren?" She looked around the group and no one spoke up.

"It's hard to think about anything else," said Roberta.

"This is still sort of about the case," began Myra, "but maybe you can give me an idea. Martha said she'd like to notify Bev's friends about her death, but she doesn't have any contact information. Did any of you notice an address book at Bev's when we packed up her things?"

"No, there was so little of a personal nature," reminded Olivia.

"I can go on her Facebook page and look at the list of her friends," said Tessa.

"How could you do that?" asked Kay.

"It's easy. I went to her page before, remember? Another idea is if Martha could give me Bev's password, or any suggestions about what a password might be, I could check out her private messaging. She might be in contact with people who aren't 'friends' but have some relationship with her."

"But there wasn't a computer at the cabin," said Wanda. "How could she have been on Facebook?"

"Maybe the police took her computer to try and find clues," suggested Kay.

"Oh, I remember when Martha and Officer Barta were talking the very first time. He asked if Bev had a computer and Martha said no. She said Bev used the computers at the library. I know the sisters emailed, and I guess she was on Facebook, too," said Myra.

"Well, I'll stop by on my way home and talk to Martha about a possible password," Tessa said.

There was silence around the table for a moment. Roberta picked up her purse. "We might as well be going. I've got a lot to do today." The others nodded and they gathered their things and left.

Tessa followed Myra home. As soon as they got out of their cars, Martha came rushing out, her face flushed. "You won't believe this!" she called to them. "That young officer called. They've declared it a murder and they've made an arrest! Bev's ex, Mike, has been arrested and charged with murder!"

CHAPTER SEVENTEEN

Tessa quickly texted Olivia and told her to get in touch with the others and get over to Myra's right away. The three women moved into Myra's living room and sat down as Martha told everything she knew.

"I couldn't believe it when he called me!" began Martha. 'He said they had ruled out an accident and probably also suicide. They had evidence that witnesses put Mike in the area that day, and even one saw him go to Bev's cabin in the evening that she died. You could have knocked me over with a feather! I never suspected Mike, not in a million years. In all the time they were together, I don't think he ever hit her. In fact, she told me that herself once."

"I'm sure he wanted to at times," said Myra, "considering the way she treated him. Maybe he finally simply snapped."

"I guess so. Oh, it breaks my heart to think she was murdered. Murdered! That's such a terrible word."

Tessa and Myra could only nod in agreement. What else was there to say?

Myra stood. "I'll fix us some tea and bring out some muffins while we're waiting for the others. I'll be right back." She turned and went into the kitchen.

"In the meantime, Martha, I think I can help you with something. At breakfast this morning Myra mentioned that you wanted some way to contact Bev's friends about her death. We could go on Facebook and look over the list of her friends. You might want to let them know."

"Oh, that would help a lot."

"And if you could give me her password, I could see who else she's been messaging and let them know, too."

"I'll bring up my laptop now and we can get right to work," said Martha, rising to go to the basement apartment.

Officer Barta sat back in the chair at his office. He felt good about being able to give Mrs. Myers some concrete information about her sister's death. Now, to get to work on all the paperwork involved.

The phone on his desk rang its shrill sound.

Grabbing up the instrument he said, "Barta, here." He listened for a moment.

"Are you sure? . . . .Uh huh . . . .And there can be no mistake? . . . .But she didn't actually die from a heart attack, right. Drowning is still the cause of death? . . . .Uh huh . . . .OK. Thanks." He ended the call and drummed his fingers on the desk. "I can't believe this," he muttered.

Picking up the phone, he punched in the number for the police chief in Angel Fire.

"Chief, it's Andy again. I know I called you last night to tell you we got the murderer. Well, here's a new twist. I just got a call from the lab. That bitter orange diet stuff I gave them? She had a huge overdose in her system. It might have been enough to kill her, but they still declare drowning as the cause of death. . . . .Yeah, that's right. . .

.So, here's the thing. I've got a murderer in jail in Albuquerque, and now this could be suicide. . . . It looks like we're back to square one."

Martha had been looking over Tessa's shoulder as the younger woman worked to get on Bev's Facebook page. They had gone over the list of friends, and now Tessa was trying passwords to be able to get into the messaging.

"Oh, here we go," said Tessa. "Let's see." She began scrolling through a large number of messages. "She liked to use this method of communication, I see. Interesting. She sent a lot of messages to her ex-husband."

"Did he ever send messages to her?" asked Martha.

Tessa shook her head as she continued to scroll through. "No, he never did. Now, this is even more interesting. She sent a couple of messages to that foster brother, Zack."

Myra came in with a plate of muffins. Setting them on the coffee table she went over and looked over Tessa's other shoulder. "That's a surprise," she said. "What did she say?"

"Oh, my gosh, listen to this! 'Zack, I found you on Facebook and see you're in Taos. I'm up at a cabin at the Bobcat Meadows RV Park between Eagle Nest and Red River. Why don't you come up and see me?'"

Martha shook her head in disbelief. "She'd never ask him to come see her. Never!"

"Did he answer?" asked Martha.

"Sure did. He said, 'Good to hear from you. I'm actually free Friday. What time should I come?'"

"I'm not believing this," said Martha.

"Then she said, 'Sounds good. Come at eight p.m. Is that this Friday, April 17th or the next?'"

The three women looked at each other, reflecting shocked expressions.

"And does he say the 17th?" Martha's voice was barely above a whisper. Her hand trembled against the chair back Tessa sat in.

Tessa nodded. "Yes."

"I'm calling Officer Barta right now." Martha got her cell phone off the table and quickly used her speed dial.

Officer Barta had been interrogating Zack Sadowsky for an hour. Immediately after Martha Myers phone call he had ordered Zack's arrest and sent two officers to search his trailer and his truck.

For perhaps the hundredth time, Zack declared his innocence and said he hadn't seen Beverly Tensley in years. A knock on the door, and an officer stuck his head in. "Can I see you for a minute?" he said.

Officer Barta followed the officer a few feet down the hall after closing the door firmly behind him. "What have you got?" he asked.

"First, his boss at the bar said Sadowsky was off the night of April 17th. That trailer is full of enough to get him on some kind of charges, drugs, maybe revenge porn or something. That guy's a filthy piece of trash. But here's the big thing." He handed Officer Barta a plastic evidence bag containing a bottle of bitter orange extract. "It had fallen under the seat in his truck. I bet the lab will find fingerprints from both that guy and the murder victim on this. And when they go over his truck, I suspect they'll find more traces."

"Bingo!" said Officer Barta, smiling. "Good work." He headed back to the interrogation room.

"I think it's time you changed your story. It will go a lot easier on you if you cooperate." He tossed the bag with the evidence on the table. "Our evidence technicians are going to find a lot more incriminating clues when they go over your truck. This plus your message on Facebook is going to make a water-tight case, my friend. So, start from the beginning and tell me everything. You're about to be charged with murder."

A look of pure panic crossed Zack's face as it drained of color. His whole body sagged. He looked about wildly as if trying to find an escape route, then looked at the pill bottle as tears came to his eyes. "It wasn't murder. It was an accident, and that's the truth. I'll tell you everything."

Officer Barta leaned back. "I've got all day. Remember, this is being recorded."

"OK, this is what happened. Out of the blue I hear from Bev. In all the years since the foster home, she never once tried to get in touch with me. I'd reached out to her lots of times, but she wouldn't give me the time of day. She was always that way, back in the home. Always looking down her nose at me as if she was better than me. No way. We were the same, her and me. Outcasts. Unwanted."

"She got in touch with you, and then?" Officer Barta nudged Zack back on the subject.

"Yeah. She asked me to come see her. And I said I'd come."

"Didn't you think it was strange that she asked you to come visit after all this time?"

"Sure, I thought it was strange. But I put myself out there on the Internet and many women ask me to come see them. So, I went there to her cabin at the time she told me."

"What time was that?"

"She said eight p.m. and that's exactly when I got there. I knock on the door, she opens it and invites me in. We go sit in her living room. No welcome hug or nothing. I sit down and there's two bottles of wine on the table and two glasses. One bottle's open and she pours me a glass of wine and hands it to me. That's all that was in the bottle, and she opens the other bottle and pours her a glass, sets it on the coffee table and says 'I'll get us some nuts.' While she goes to the little kitchen area to get the nuts, I switch the glasses. I mean, like it's rude to give your guest the old wine, right? I wanted the fresh wine. Who knew how long that other bottle had been open. I'm a bartender, you know. I know wine that's been open for days isn't as good."

Officer Barta gestured for Zack to keep going.

"OK, so we sit and talk for a while, the usual small talk people do, and we're drinking that wine. I figure she asked me to come see her because she was wanting some action, you know what I mean? We're both sitting on the couch, and I reach over and start to touch her, you know, warming her up. She jumps away from me like I was poison. She starts pacing around saying all this bad stuff about me from when we were in the foster home. That really made me mad. I mean, what did that have to do with anything anymore. I get up too, and we get to arguing. She starts cussing me and shoving me. Well, I don't take that kind of stuff from nobody, so I start shoving back. I try to grab her and get something started again, but she slaps my face and calls me a disgusting animal. Then she says, 'You can't ever hurt anyone again because I put something in your drink that will make you have a major heart attack. I know you have a bad heart and that has ephedra in it.' She pulls this bottle of capsules out of her pocket and shakes them in my face. 'You're going to be dead soon and it will look natural so I'll never be charged with murder.' When she said that I about went crazy. Then I realized the joke was on her. I started laughing in her face. I had switched the glasses. What a joke, huh?"

"Then what happened?"

"I don't know. She really lost it then after I told her the joke was on her, slapping and kicking at me. It got rougher and rougher. All of sudden when I pushed her, she lost her balance and fell back and cracked her head on the coffee table."

Zack stopped talking and wiped his mouth on his sleeve. "See. It was only an accident. Actually, it might even be considered self-defense 'cause she started it. And all along, she had planned it to kill me."

"What happened after she hit her head?"

"Nothing happened. She was lying there, dead. I knew I had to get rid of the body, but first I washed up the glasses and took the bottles in a bag out to my truck to throw away, far, far away. I knew if the body got found there and I got tied to it in some way, I wouldn't stand a chance with my record, even though this wasn't my fault. Even though it was an accident."

"Then what did you do?"

"I went back in and looked around and saw that bottle of pills, so I grabbed it up. Then I picked Bev up - she always was a tiny girl - and carried her out to the truck and put her in the passenger side. Nobody was around, but even if they had been I figured they might think she was drunk or something. I wasn't sure what to do with her, but I drove by Eagle Nest Lake and thought about dropping her in the lake. That's a busy lake, though, so I decided to haul her over to Monte Verde Lake instead. When I got to that area where they keep the boats, there'd been so much water that the boats were starting to float out into the lake. I stuck her under one of them canoes. I figured it'd take her to the middle of the lake before too long. Then all my worries would be over. I forgot about the pills. They must have fallen under the seat when I was putting her in the truck."

Zack sat back, looking drained. "So, that's the whole story, Officer. It was an accident, and I panicked. Looking back, I guess I should have called 911 and said someone had fallen and hit their head."

"That would have been a lot better for both you and Bev. You see, she wasn't dead then. She didn't die until she drowned in the lake." He motioned to the two police officers standing by the door. "Read him his rights and book him for murder. I've got to go let someone else out of jail."

CHAPTER EIGHTEEN

The next Tuesday morning the JULIETs were a quiet group. They placed their orders and talked about the weather until they were served.

"Well, we did it," Myra finally said. "We really did it. The Snoop Sisters are the ones who got the murder solved."

"Yes, but what started out as something exciting and fun, ended as, I don't know, depressing and awful. I don't want the JULIETs to be Snoop Sisters anymore," said Roberta.

Wanda agreed. "Me, neither. It got me feeling so low I couldn't find a funny tee shirt to wear today."

"It was interesting, and I'm glad we could use our ingenuity to help Officer Barta. Even so, I'll be glad to get back to being simply the JULIETs again," said Tessa.

Each of the group nodded their agreement.

"Martha was so appreciative of everything we did. I can't imagine what would have happened if we hadn't gotten involved," Myra said.

Kay looked at Myra. "What happens now?"

"Before the Myers left, Martha told me that eventually there will be a trial. Exactly what the outcome of that trial will be is up to the lawyers, the judge, and the jury. But, no matter what it is, there is no doubt that Zack Sadowsky will be behind bars."

"How tragic that Bev's death could have been avoided. I mean that Zack thought she was already dead when she wasn't," commented Olivia.

Wanda set down her coffee cup. "And look how many lives were affected by all this. I'm thinking of Ted and all your family, Roberta, and then Jeremy, and that ex-husband Mike Tensley."

Roberta nodded. "It has really bruised our family, but we're a strong unit. I think we'll come out OK. Ted and Mindy are trying so hard to rebuild what they had. I'm sure it never can be the same, but we pray they can be a family unit again, especially for the boys' sake."

Annabelle touched Roberta's hand. "I think that's a good possibility." She smiled at her friend. She turned to Kay. "And Jeremy. What's going on with him?"

"I think it's a day-by-day thing. Ben is working hard to help that boy, and I believe he can do it. He wants to keep Jeremy from going into the foster care system and being moved around from home to home until he turns eighteen, and then simply released on his own with no resources. Ben is determined to help Jeremy get a GED degree and get some direction for his life."

Myra grinned. "But won't having Jeremy with him all the time cramp his courting time with you, Kay?"

"Myra! For heaven's sake. There is no 'courting'. We're friends, good friends, and that's all we're interested in being." All the JULIETs smiled at Kay and noted her slight blush. They were a lot happier with their usual style of teasing than continuing to talk about Bev Tensley.

"Speaking of foster care, Tessa, how's your application process coming to be foster parents?" asked Roberta.

"We're ready for the home inspection visits to get finished up; then we'll decide. We want to be foster parents very badly, but we're also a little afraid of the commitment."

"That's the thing about life, isn't it?" said Annabelle. "Those things that could be the most rewarding require the most risk. It's a scary thing to risk our hearts, to open ourselves to someone else. It's like our friendship. When we come together, we not only share a meal. We share ourselves."

"And what would we do without each other?" asked Roberta.

The six friends held their cups up to each other in silent commitment.

As they set them down, Wanda said, "I'm sure I can find a tee shirt for that."

The sound of their shared laughter filled the coffee shop and they carried the echo with them when they left.

RECIPES FROM THE JULIETS' COOKBOOK

APPETIZERS

RASPBERRY SALSA (or salsa of your choice)
(Submitted by D.J. Geoffroy)

1 pkg cream cheese
Can of black beans, drained
Bag of tortilla chips
Salsa
Place cream cheese in baking dish. Pour beans over top, then pour salsa over top. Bake at 350 degrees for 30 minutes.
Serve with chips to dip.

SWEET AND SPICY SMOKIES
(Submitted by MaryBeth Maxwell)

1pkg little smokies
1/2 cup brown sugar
1 tsp chili powder - or more if you like it hot
10 strips bacon cut into thirds
Toothpicks
Wrap bacon around smokie & secure with toothpick.
Put in bowl filled with sugar & chili powder that has been mixed
Continue till finish all smokies
Cover & place in fridge over night or a few days
Put smokies on foil covered baking pan
Bake about 30 min. at 350
Take out & serve.

If left overs remain, put in fridge. Microwave a minute or so to warm up

BAKED SPINACH AND ARTICHOKE DIP
(Submitted by Suzanne Coyle)

2 -6 oz pkgs of fresh baby spinach
1 tbsp butter
1 -8 oz pkg 1/3 less fat cream cheese
1 garlic clove, chopped
1 - 14 oz can artichoke hearts, drained & chopped
½ cup light sour cream
½ cup shredded part mozzarella cheese, divided
Fresh pita wedges or baked pita chips

Microwave spinach in a large microwave-safe bowl 3 min or until wilted. Drain spinach well, pressing between paper towels. Chop spinach.

Melt butter in a non-stick skillet over high heat. Add cream cheese and garlic. Cook 3 – 6 min stirring constantly until cream cheese melts. Fold in spinach, artichokes, sour cream and ¼ cup mozzarella cheese. Stir until cheese melts.

Transfer mixture to a 1 quart shallow baking dish. Sprinkle with remaining ¼ cup mozzarella cheese.

Bake at 350 degrees for 15 min or until hot and bubbly.

Serve immediately with pita wedges or chips.

ENTREES

SPINACH-GREEN CHILI LASAGNA
(Submitted by Carolin Sanders)

1 8oz pkg no boil Lasagna noodles
2 15oz cans Hatch Green Chili Sauce
3 Cups grated mozzarella cheese
15oz Ricotta Cheese
1/2 cup fresh Parmesan cheese grated
2 eggs
1 tbsp Italian seasoning
4 or more cups fresh spinach, cut up
3 or 4 mild green chilies sliced, seeded

Mix eggs seasonings, and cheeses. Layer ingredients beginning with sauce then lasagna, cheese mixture, spinach, chilies. Repeat. Sprinkle a little Parmesan on top before baking at 350 degrees covered for 30-40 minutes or till done. Be sure to have at least 4 cups of liquid (chicken stock or water) if you use the whole package noodles. Enjoy. Can be put together the day ahead then baked.

HAM LOAF
(Originally from Laura Vance)

1 ½ lb ham, ground
½ lb pork, ground
1 cup cracker crumbs
2 eggs
1 cup milk

Sauce:
1 ½ cup brown sugar
½ cup vinegar
½ cup water
¼ cup dry mustard

Mix and form into a loaf. Stick with cloves and baste with sauce. Bake at 300 degrees for 2 hours.

CHICKEN POT PIE
(A Myra Stanhope casserole)

4 cups cubed chicken
1 lb sausage
1 stick butter
Flour
Salt, pepper
Chicken stock
10 oz pkg frozen peas, defrosted
Milk
Refrigerated pie crust
Caraway seeds

Brown sausage in skillet. Set aside.
In the same skillet melt butter. Stir in flour, salt and pepper until smooth. Add milk and/or chicken stock and stir until smooth.

Mix together chicken, sausage, peas, and cream sauce until well blended. Pour into a 13x 9 baking dish. Cover with pie crust sprinkled with caraway seeds.

Bake at 350 degrees for 30 min or until crust is lightly browned and ingredients are hot and bubbly.

BREADS

FIESTA CORN BAKE
(Submitted by Karen Pettersen)

1/2 cup sour cream dip (French onion, chives or ranch)
2 cans Fiesta Whole Kernel Corn (drained)
1 tbsp. flour
1 tsp. sugar

Stir together dip, flour, sugar. Add corn.
Spoon into 1-quart casserole dish. Sprinkle with broken corn chips or cheese-flavored crackers.
Bake, uncovered, at 375 F, 30 minutes or until heated through.
Prep time: 5 minutes; Cook time: 30 minutes.
Serves 4

MORNING GLORY MUFFINS
(Originally a Joann Wright recipe from The Copper Steamer Published by Martha Lassetter and submitted via Linda Nelson)

2 ½ cups flour
2 tsps baking powder
¼ tsp salt
2 tsps cinnamon
1 cup brown sugar and 1 cup granulated sugar
3 sticks butter, softened
3 eggs
2 tsps vanilla
3 cups chopped nuts
1 cup chopped nuts
½ cup crushed pineapple, undrained

Preheat oven to 350 degrees. Combine 1st 5 ingredients. Add butter, eggs, vanilla. Mix well. Add 3 cups chopped nuts and pineapple. Pour batter into lined muffin tins. Top with remaining nuts.

Bake at 350 degrees for:

Mini muffins – 15 – 20 minutes; standard, 20 – 22 min; jumbo – 20 – 28 minutes.

Will last for days in the refrigerator.

BEST KOLACHE DOUGH
(Submitted by Jacqueline Covey)

2 pkgs dry yeast
¼ cup lukewarm water
2 cups milk, scalded
¼ cup sugar
2tsp salt
1 cup butter
6 egg yolks
6cups flour

In small bowl, dissolve yeast in lukewarm water. In mixing bowl, cream butter, sugar, and salt. Add egg yolks one at a time, beating well after each addition. Stir in milk and cool to lukewarm before adding yeast mixture. Beat in flour. Place in greased bowl, cover and let rise until double in bulk. Punch down and turn out half of dough onto floured board. Roll to ¾ inch thickness and cut with biscuit cutter. Place on a greased cookie sheet one inch apart. Brush with melted butter. Let rise until double and then press out center to hold filling. Fill with prune, poppy seed, apricot, filling etc. and let rise again. Bake at 475 degrees for 8-10 minutes.

VEGETABLES/SIDE DISHES

CAULIFLOWER PIQUANT
(Submitted by Valerie Byrd)

1 medium head cauliflower
3 Tbs. hot water
1/2 cup low fat mayonnaise
1 tsp. salt
1 tbsp prepared Dijon mustard
1/2 cup sharp cheddar cheese, shredded
Paprika

Cook whole cauliflower in salted water for 20 minutes till tender (but not mushy!). Combine the remaining ingredients and, after draining the cauliflower, spread the cheese mixture on top and bake in oven 10-15 minutes until golden brown. Sprinkle lightly with paprika.

Note: I add Vietnamese garlic hot sauce or Tabasco for extra flavor...and usually forget to sprinkle the paprika, but it works!

SPINACH RISOTTO
(Submitted by June Rau)

5 cups chicken broth
2 tsp olive oil
½ of a medium onion, finely chopped
1 clove of garlic, minced
1 1/2 tsp dried oregano
1 cup Arborio rice
2 cups finely chopped spinach

3 tbsp dry white wine
¼ cup grated Parmesan cheese

Bring chicken broth to a boil in medium saucepan, then reduce heat to low.

Heat a wide and relatively deep saucepan over medium heat for several minutes and then add the oil. After an additional minute, add onion and garlic. Cook for 4 min, stirring frequently. Add the oregano, rice and spinach. Stir until the rice is coated with oil. Add the wine and cook until it has almost completely evaporated.

Add about 1 cup of the hot broth and stir constantly until the rice has absorbed most of it. Continue to add broth, about 1 cup at a time, until all the broth is gone or the rice becomes chewy and tender, and is not chalk white in the center. It is important to stir frequently so the rice doesn't stick to the pan.

Once the rice is done, stir in the Parmesan cheese and serve immediately.

COPPER PENNIES
(Submitted by Joan Bohls)

2 pounds carrots scrapped, sliced like pennies and salted
1 mild onion
1 can tomato soup
1/2 cup olive oil
3/4 cup rice vinegar
1/4 cup sugar
1 tsp mustard
1 tsp Worcestershire sauce

Cook carrots in salted water. When done, drain and layer carrots in a pretty glass bowl alternating with thinly sliced onion rings. Mix soup, oil, sugar, Worcestershire sauce, vinegar and mustard. Pour mixture over vegetables and marinate over night. Serve cold. Enjoy!

DESSERTS

POTS DE CRÈME
(Submitted by Sandra Miller)

1 egg
2 tbsp sugar
Dash salt
¾ cup half-and-half cream
1 cup (6oz) semisweet chocolate chips
1 tsp vanilla extract
Can serve with raspberries or other fruit and whipped cream

In a small saucepan, combine the egg, sugar and salt. Whisk in cream. Cook and stir over medium heat until mixture reaches 160° and coats the back of a metal spoon.

Remove from the heat; whisk in chocolate chips and vanilla until smooth. Pour into small dessert dishes. Cover and refrigerate for 8 hours or overnight. Garnish with whipped cream if desired.

SWEEDISH ALMOND BARS
(Myra Stanhope's favorite cookie recipe)

1 cup sliced almonds, divided
1 cup butter or margarine
4 large eggs
2 cups sugar
1 ½ to 2 tsp almond extract
¼ tsp lemon extract
2 ½ cups all-purpose flour

½ tsp salt
3 tbsp sugar
¼ tsp ground cinnamon

Sprinkle ½ cup almonds in bottom of greased 15x10 inch jellyroll pan.

Beat butter and next 4 ingredients at medium speed until blended. Add flour and salt, beating until smooth; spread batter in prepared pan.

Combine sugar and cinnamon; sprinkle evenly over cookie dough. Top with remaining ½ cup almonds.

Bake at 325 degrees for 30 min or until lightly browned. Cool and cut into bars.Yield: about 4 dozen

RASPBERRY PIE
(from the Salman Raspberry Ranch
Submitted by Jan Saunders)

4-5 cups fresh or defrosted raspberries
¾ to 1 cup sugar
¼ tsp salt
2 tsp cinnamon
1 tbsp lemon juice
2-3 tbsp tapioca
½ cup butter, sliced in slivers
Refrigerated pie crusts

Place one crust in a 9 or 10 inch pie plate.

Mix ingredients and place in crust.

Place a second crust on top and press edges with a fork.

Cut slits in pie crust and bake for 35-40 min. Cool and serve

Made in the USA
Charleston, SC
25 June 2016